MYSTERY
AT OCTOBER HOUSE

Westminster Press Books by
MARJORY HALL

Mystery at October House

The April Ghost

The Other Girl

The Carved Wooden Ring

Beneath Another Sun

The Gold-lined Box

MYSTERY
AT
OCTOBER HOUSE

by Marjory Hall

The Westminster Press
Philadelphia

Published by The Westminster Press®

Philadelphia, Pennsylvania

Printed in the United States of America

Library of Congress Cataloging in Publication Data

Hall, Marjory, 1908–
Mystery at October House.

SUMMARY: Few of the guests at October House are as handsome and mysterious as Darien Richards and have his keen interest in the old Indian mounds nearby.
[1. Georgia—History—1775–1865—Fiction.
2. Mystery and detective stories] I. Title.
PZ7.H1465Mv   [Fic]   76–46565
ISBN 0–664–32606–4

Contents

1

The Dashing Stranger

I suppose at first I had no idea that the man on the big black horse was anything out of the ordinary when he rode up to October House. I had been urging Sugar and Spice, Cottie's twin grandsons, to hurry with the sweeping of the wide porch, and because they were both mischievous and lazy, I had my hands full. Sugar—even Cottie admits she named them the wrong way around—had invented a little game that involved swooping about on the broad wooden planks with his broom of twigs and branches, and then whirling himself about so vigorously that he became, or pretended to become, dizzy. Spice, the meeker of the two, watched his twin and giggled approvingly. I could, of course, have done the sweeping in half the time myself, but Uncle Simon had made it clear that the younger children were to begin to work, to earn their keep.

"Once they're trained, they will be useful, Phillis," he said—optimistically, I thought. "You can then withdraw your supervision, merely looking in on their efforts unexpectedly now and then."

For about the fiftieth time I snapped at Sugar and he, wearying of the game, I suppose, began to sweep in earnest. Spice too. Their young black faces, so alike, were almost expressionless as they plied their brooms, and with a sigh of relief I saw that they would, after all, finish the task so that I could hurry off to help

Carolina in the kitchen. It was one of those rare periods when the Inn had few guests, and at such moments we always seized the opportunity to clean the kitchen and pantries thoroughly. In order to have the work done properly, we found we must do it ourselves. Cottie is a good cook, and she works hard and well, but she seems to be a stranger to soap and water. A bowl she had mixed pudding in would stand on the bench forever, or at least until the next time she wanted it, and then often enough the pudding remaining in the bowl would find itself stirred up with the biscuits. So we had to watch her, look about the kitchen each night after she had walked wearily down to her cabin, and clean up. Still, the place needed a good turning out now and then, and this was the day we had elected for the chore. I dreaded it, but I wanted to get at it, get it over with.

It was pleasant that day in 1828. We had had a spell of beautiful weather, warm for Georgia in May, but with a breeze lurking always in the new green leaves overhead. The fact that we had not many guests annoyed Uncle Simon very much indeed, but Carolina and I were glad of the respite, taking time from our everyday work to sew, to dye a faded frock, to sit luxuriously with idle hands for as much as five minutes at a time. It would have been, I thought wistfully, a moment to talk things over—October House, Uncle Simon, ourselves, our future, if we had such a thing— but my cousin Carolina was not given to conversation. As she stitched or stirred or churned, you knew that her mind was working busily. Busily, but in secret. What did she think about? I wondered fretfully. Was she wishing herself away from isolated October House, into some town, perhaps, where she could walk down a street and talk to people, linger in the shade of a tree or the door of a shop and discuss the doctor's new wife, or the house being built next door to the church? None of my efforts to discover what went on in her mind produced results. She would murmur yes or no, sometimes answer a question with a whole sentence, but she never gave any of herself to me. I knew my cousin Carolina as little as I knew Uncle Simon (who was Carolina's uncle but not mine), and that was not at all. Perhaps Carolina, being twenty-six to my sixteen, had outgrown any desire to see the world, to have things happen. In ten years no doubt I too would forget that there was a world out there beyond the fences and the forests that bounded October House. For that matter, October House was a world in itself, huge, solitary, self-contained.

I looked around critically.

"Very well, boys. Finish up that corner there and then bring the brooms to the kitchen." They looked at me, brown eyes full of relief at being dismissed from labor, freed at last to return to their play, whatever that might be. I saw them running around all day, working off excess energy, but had no idea if their running had plot or plan to it. I sighed, rubbed my back, and turned away, heading for Carolina and the kitchen.

At that moment I heard the hoofbeats of a horse cantering through the strip of trees where countless guests had worn a narrow track from the post road to the inn. Spice hurled his broom vaguely in my direction, and rushed to the mounting block. The identical twins were different in one respect only—Spice was a fanatic about horses and voluntarily scuttled about the stable and, as now, attended to the mounting block whenever he had a chance. Sugar, bent on his own freedom, also tossed his broom away and disappeared.

Any interruption in a dull round of everyday duties is welcome. I watched the horse and its rider appear at the foot of the slope. He had clearly been on the road for some time. His clothing was covered with dust and his horse quite obviously tired, but he was a dashing figure all the same. His coat seemed to be made of soft leather, and I would not have been surprised to see a plume adorning his wide-brimmed hat. His face was bronzed by the sun, and I found myself looking into the brightest blue eyes I had ever seen. He held my eyes with his as he stepped down on the block and tossed the reins to Spice, telling him curtly that he would be out to the stable directly and see to the horse himself. I felt my foolish heart racing madly. My prayers had been answered, at last. Now my life was beginning. . . .

I found out in the first minute of our meeting that I could count on nothing, at least as far as this handsome stranger was concerned. Confidently I waited, ready to lead him to the official office, the one where guests must go to pay and to be assigned to their quarters. This was nothing more than a high desk in the passageway, since Uncle Simon's private office was his alone and guests were not welcome in it. But the bright-blue eyes that had locked with mine moved abruptly away, and the man himself, jumping lightly, for all his size, from the mounting block, strode away purposefully toward the office as though he had been doing it all of his life. I knew well enough he had never been at October House before. I could never forget *him.*

Numbly I turned in the opposite direction and walked in a sort of haze down the wooden steps to the kitchen. Carolina, a kerchief tied around her sandy hair and wearing her most voluminous and also oldest apron, was scrubbing away at one of the long wooden tables. She looked at me as my shadow darkened the door and said, "Took you long enough. Where are the brooms?"

Wordlessly I hurried back, my eyes fixed on the doorway through which the stranger had disappeared. Who could have remembered a broom at such a time? And yet we must always be careful of all our tools and implements. The servants would not steal them. They did not even borrow them for their own use. With the exception of a few pitiful little gardens scratched out haphazardly around their cabins, they had no personal use for tools of any kind. But Spice or Sugar or one of the other children, seeing a broom or hoe lying about, would seize it and turn it into a horse to ride madly around one field after the other, or a spear to hurl mightily into a tangled thicket, and then abandon it. After a fruitless search, we would set Job, Cottie's partially paralyzed husband, to making a new broom of twigs and branches, or smoothing a handle for the hoe blade the blacksmith would hammer out for us. It was simpler, in the long run, to keep one's hands on things.

I put the brooms in their allotted corner and joined Carolina at her work. For once I didn't mind her lack of conversation, because I felt like thinking. I wanted to remember that handsome bronze face, the dashing wide-brimmed hat, the high boots covered with dust that yet somehow conveyed the impression of polish underneath.

As soon as we had scoured the kitchen, cobblestone floor and all, to Carolina's satisfaction, we went to our room under the eaves of the weaving shed and changed our clothes. Carolina had made a rule about that. Since we were sometimes required to help serve at supper, or in other ways appear before the guests, we should at such times look presentable, as became the members of Uncle Simon's family. I rebelled often enough, feeling that if I were to be drudge and servant girl I might as well dress like one. But tonight I changed gladly. In fact, I would have put on my best frock, which was not grand at all but was still my finest, if I thought Carolina would countenance it. She wouldn't, of course, and what's more she would have asked questions. How astonished she would be, I thought, if she knew that for the first time since I had been at October House I found myself interested in a guest.

As soon as I could I slipped through the dining hall and went to the passage. Five saddles hung on their pegs. Only five—no wonder Uncle Simon was glum. This meant that each guest would have a bed of his own. We can accommodate twelve or so in this fashion, but as soon as there are more, the men must double up in the beds placed around the three big bedrooms. Sometimes we have as many as four to a bed, but no one complains. That is common enough on the rough roads, even in 1828.

But at the moment I was concerned with only one of the saddles hanging there, and I had no trouble identifying the one I was interested in. Besides, there above it was the dashing hat. I looked at it, wondering if I dared take it down and brush it, but knew I did not. The saddle, at any rate, had been well cared for. I wondered which room and bed had been assigned to the handsome stranger. More than that, I wondered what his name was. No one was about, since it wanted nearly an hour to suppertime, so I sidled over to the high desk. The book was open on it, the book in which Uncle Simon wrote, in his spidery hand, the names of the guests as they arrived, and in some calligraphy of his own the money received from each, often with little notes concerning the length of stay, I supposed, or perhaps information on a man's business or his possible return. I had never cared before, but I cared now.

The last name on the somewhat ruffled page should, I felt, have been written in fire. Instead, in black ink I saw inscribed: "Darien Richards," together with squiggly figures and hieroglyphs. Darien, I thought, what a dashing name! And suitable. Darien!

I disliked being called upon to wait on table, but would have given anything I owned to perform that duty that night. But no, Cottie was feeling poorly, and Carolina ordered that she and I would take Cottie's place in the kitchen. At the moment there were plenty of young girls about who could serve. Cottie alone had three daughters—one being the mother of Sugar and Spice, the other two younger and unmarried—and for five travelers that was all that was needed.

I swallowed my resentment as best I could and tried to comfort myself that this very slice of meat falling on the chopping board under my knife might go onto Darien's plate, that one of the biscuits I had just taken fresh and hot from the brick oven would be buttered by his hand. If only I understood Uncle Simon's peculiar marks and symbols, I could have told how long he might stay, although few of them stay for more than one night. There is little enough business in the neighborhood of the village of Oktobee Falls, where October House is. Tomorrow he would ride away, probably to the mountains, I thought, feeling clever, because the dust that had covered him and his mount was most likely acquired on the plain to the east.

Sometimes I could hear laughter from over my head

as the men ate their supper, and twice Sukey, Cottie's youngest daughter, came running down the stairs to the kitchen in a fit of giggles.

"Funny," she said, rolling her eyes upward. "Very funny, that big man. There, hear them now?" she added, as a burst of laughter surged above us.

"That big man" could only mean Darien. Our guests often laughed at table, but not so much as to-night. I glared at Sukey, because she heard his words and stories, saw him, even touched him perhaps as she put down his plate of ham and beans and greens, passed him the platter of steaming biscuits. I did not so much as know the color of his hair, since the jaunty sweep of the broad brim had hidden it from me, but Sukey did. I could not endure it!

As soon as I could, I escaped from the kitchen and hurried upstairs. If someone had stopped me to ask what I was doing, I would have been unable to think of an answer. Unless called upon for some special task, Carolina and I never entered the big house after we had cleaned up the supper things, with the exception of the most blustery nights in winter, when the small fireplace in the weaving shed could not chase away the waves of bitter cold that swept down from the mountains. Then we used Uncle Simon's private office—his real office, where accounts were kept and lists made, orders written for supplies not procurable in Oktobee Falls. Until it was time to go to bed in the chilly shed, Carolina and I were welcome to sit in the stiff, uncomfortable room with our sewing. The chairs were hard and much too straight, and the flickering light of the candles Uncle Simon somewhat grudgingly lighted for us made sewing and knitting difficult, so we never lingered long. That, no doubt, was part of his plan.

Normally I would now go to the weaving shed,

where each day we made a space for ourselves among the looms and spindles and spinning wheels, to sew or read a little until the light faded, but tonight I was filled with rebellion. Darien Richards was somewhere in the House, and I wanted to see him again, regardless of the consequences. A reprimand from Uncle Simon would not harm me, but not seeing the newcomer again that day would, most decidedly.

I found him, oddly enough, sitting by himself on the bottom step of the stairway leading to the upstairs rooms from the passage next the dining hall. The other men were standing around the fireplace at one end of the dining hall, drinking coffee. Sukey and her sister Ellie, had cleared the table and left the urn and mugs behind. Why, I wondered, did one man leave the group and seat himself on a stairway, shut off from talk and fire and good hot coffee?

He looked up as I walked through the door. In the dim light I saw that his eyes were bluer than any sky I had ever seen, and that his hair, which was thick and curly, was black as night. And then I remembered where I was and that I should not be there and began to back hastily away.

"Don't leave," he said. "I would like to talk to you. Here, sit down by me."

He moved over, and I sat down as one in a trance. What would have happened if Uncle Simon had wandered into the hallway I have no idea, and at the time worried about such a thing not one whit. I sat down, looked up at him, and found myself smiling into his eyes.

"That's better. You know, a man on the road all the time, he sees many men like himself. And becomes bored with them, unhappily. There are too few pretty girls along the way, far too few, so when I see one I wish to take advantage. I hoped you would come this way," he added gravely, and my heart jumped. He had thought of me, waited for me even!

"Now," he went on, "tell me about yourself. Beginning with your name. Mine is Darien Richards. And yours?"

"Phillis Randolph," I told him. I was surprised that my voice sounded normal. It might very well have come out a sort of a croak, or even have suddenly found itself entirely without sound.

"The old gentleman who—who took my money," he said with a wry smile, "would be your grandfather? His name is Randolph too? Or no, I thought he told me another name—Browning, could it be?"

I found myself telling him everything, about my parents' death when I was a baby, about how Carolina, already orphaned and taken in by Uncle Simon, heard about me, and had me found and brought to October House although but ten herself, about our work, all of it. He listened as though it was a thrilling story, and with the most flattering attention asked me a question now and then—who stopped here, how many could we handle at one time, what in general was the business of the guests who patronized October House?

It was not until the next day that I realized he had perhaps been more interested in his fellow travelers than in us. But no matter. Why should I care as long as I had the memory of sitting at the bottom of the stairway talking to him? It was the most blissful experience of my life.

Darien Richards soon made himself prominent in our small world. He talked to the servants, who smiled and nodded and laughed at him. He talked to the guests, one by one, easily and with courtesy. I saw him twice in deep conversation with Mr. Comstock, the plump little man who passed our way twice a year, carrying with him an assortment of sundries which he brought up from the coast and sold to the folk living in the mountains far from the centers where such goods could be found. He did well enough at it, I gathered, since his clothes were always of the finest, and his fat white hands wore flashing rings, like a woman's. They seemed deep in earnest conversation, but I could not hear a word. Later, though, I heard Mr. Comstock tell Mr. Beedle about his talk with Darien.

"That Richards fella as just came," he said, while I lurked in the passageway, anxious to hear every syllable that had to do with Darien, "says he is interested in antiques. He'll be here awhile. Might be a customer for you, Beedle."

Mr. Beedle snorted. "More like a competitor," he said morosely. "All at once the country is filled with people who find it expedient to buy chairs from one person's attic and place them in another person's parlor."

"Ah, well," said Mr. Comstock blandly, "everyone has by now recovered from the upstart war with those British rascals, and survived the panic that followed. Time they thought about improving their lot a bit. Why, even up in the high valleys I find—" The rest was lost on me because the men moved away to the dining hall and I could not go after them.

The most important thing was that Darien was staying on at October House "awhile." Mr. Beedle, who had later had his talk with Darien, at some of which I managed to be present, announced that he was moving westward earlier than he had planned.

"Afraid of Richards, I believe," I heard Mr. Comstock say to the new man who had arrived just that morning. "Beedle both buys and sells as he goes, you understand, and he usually rests here for several days, mapping out his journey."

"Why should he be afraid of Richards?" asked the newcomer, whom I disliked on sight. He had a face like a ferret, pointed and inquisitive, and his voice matched it, sharp and insistent. His name was Amos Byers, and both Carolina and I, who paid little enough attention to the guests as a rule and seldom discussed them, could find nothing good to say of him.

"He stood by me while I helped Sukey churn," Carolina complained, "and asked me questions, one a minute."

"Me too. Why should he care about us, or how many travelers we have in a year? I'd like to see him try that with Uncle Simon. He'd send him packing."

"He's too shrewd for that," Carolina admitted. "He asked me point-blank what Mr. Comstock did, and Mr. Richards, and had we ever seen Mr. Plumb or Mr. Richards before this year—things like that. Little enough he got from me."

I had at first been curious about Carolina's reaction to Darien, but it was plain that she saw him as just another mouth to feed. How she could miss his devastating charm I couldn't imagine, but then I had never understood Carolina. I waited now outside the door, having learned to make myself into a shadow or piece of furniture whenever I wanted to, to see what Mr. Comstock had to say.

"Richards is interested in Beedle's line, I believe," Mr. Comstock said idly.

"Which is?"

"What? Oh, Beedle goes about looking for old furniture, stuff made in England primarily, he told me, which is common enough up north and down on the coast, but in short supply here."

"You mean," Mr. Byers inquired, "that he carries such pieces with him? But he had a horse only, no wagon, that I could see."

Amos Byers, I reflected, saw a great deal.

"He has a sort of folio with him, with sketches, I believe." Mr. Comstock was clearly bored with the inquisition. He would soon, I knew, start talking about the contents of his own saddlebags, making them sound as alluring as possible. "He shows the sketches, takes orders, and then when he returns to wherever he is from—Maryland, I believe—he fills the orders from his stock there or hunts about for the pieces required and ships them as he finds them."

"H'mm," said Mr. Byers. "But how does Richards fit into that?"

"Oh, he doesn't, he doesn't," Mr. Comstock said testily. "I just said that I thought Richards was interested in furniture and mentioned it to Beedle. I didn't mean to frighten the man away."

"*Is* Richards interested in furniture?"

"Good gracious, man, go ask him yourself. *I* don't know. I met him only two days ago, and he happened to say he had an interest in old things. He was asking questions too, almost as many as you do, sir," and he marched away, looking more than ever like a plump pigeon with ruffled feathers.

That didn't stop Mr. Byers from asking questions, though. He talked to one after another, always steering clear of Uncle Simon, however, and I never happened to spy him talking to Darien. But he must have. For my part, I flew around the place like one possessed. If Carolina was surprised at my zeal in running errands, she didn't show it. Or if she noticed that sometimes I was very slow in returning, she made no mention. All I wanted was to be where Darien was as much as possible. The fact that he rode out each morning and was gone several hours disappointed me, but at least I knew that sooner or later he'd be back in October House again. That any day now he would leave us, and for good, I refused to think about.

It was during this period that strange things began to happen. Nothing large, nothing important in itself. Mystifying, more like. I myself happened to be concerned with the first one. Uncle Simon had long since established a post office in October House. It was a logical thing to do, because of the north-south road that followed the Oktobee River just east of us, and the east-west post road that brought travelers to us, as well as mail that was usually carried on the stagecoach or sometimes by a post rider. The post office itself consisted of twenty-four pigeonholes in a honeycomb of dark wood. People from around Oktobee Falls rode in now and then to find letters in their pigeonholes and to pay Uncle Simon for them, or to leave letters to go out on the next stage. It was a nuisance, Uncle Simon complained, to collect the fees owed on letters, and he said often enough that someday the Government would see the wisdom of charging for a letter before it was sent, instead of when received. That, of course, would be impossible, since a letter was paid for according to the distance it had traveled, but he stubbornly believed in a uniform charge for all, whether a letter was sent from Georgia to Massachusetts, or only to another town in Georgia.

One of the chores I almost liked about the place was sorting the mail. I seemed to travel, in a sense, as I handled letters written in far-off places by unknown people to persons I might or might not know. I knew where they should be put, each travel-stained rectangle, and I felt very deft and knowledgeable as I popped them quickly into their rightful cubbyholes.

On this lovely morning in late May I took the sack brought up from the stage by a newly arriving guest, peered about me to make sure that Darien's saddle and wide hat were gone from their pegs, and began to sort. Without looking I put two official-appearing letters into Mr. Quarrie's box, and encountered resistance. Mr. Quarrie received more mail than anyone else in the county, I was sure, and he sent someone over every few days to collect what there was for him and to pay the slip that Uncle Simon had put in his box. Mr. Quarrie's man had come yesterday, so there should be nothing there now, I knew that much, and I reached up to find out what it was that was interfering with my work.

My fingers touched something cool and smooth. It was not, I sensed at once, a letter, but rather an object made of metal. I pulled it out and looked with amazement at a disk formed in copper, with an intricate but primitive design sketched on its surface. It had been cleaned a little so that the pinkish metal glowed here and there. One edge had been pierced, as though a string might be put through it. It could, I thought, be worn as a locket, although it had a forbidding look to it, somehow, and it was overlarge for a piece of jewelry.

Who would put such a thing there? And why? Uncle Simon was very strict about people taking advantage of the post office and putting it to some use of their own. The Hawleys, our nearest neighbors, had for a time thought it a convenient—and free—way to communicate with their daughter, who was married to Sterling Phillips and lived up the river a mile or so, but when Uncle Simon found a meat pie tucked somewhat sloppily into their pigeonhole there had been a fine to-do, and the Hawleys, at any rate, never tried such a thing again. Perhaps someone had put this copper disk there for Mr. Quarrie, so I decided not to get myself in the middle of something unpleasant. Instead of taking it to Uncle Simon as I first planned, I put it back and carefully placed the letters on top of it. Mr. Quarrie was a politician, which meant that he meddled in many people's affairs. But it would be unwise, I decided, to meddle in his in any fashion.

So that was the first thing. I expected some sort of stir when Mr. Quarrie had the disk delivered to him with his mail, but since there was none I decided I had been right, and it had been intended for him after all. It simply surprised me that Mr. Quarrie would disobey Uncle Simon's rigid rule in such a manner. Mr. Quarrie, as I have said, was a politician, and took care to offend no one.

Anyway, I had better things to think of. Darien sought me out the very next day and asked me to go for a walk with him.

"My horse has gone a little lame," he explained. "I'm leaving him in the stable for a day or two so he will be ready to travel."

"Travel!" My heart stopped. But of course it had to come, and it would not be for a day or two, at any rate.

"So," he went on, "I thought to explore on foot. This is very beautiful country hereabout, and I like looking at it. But I need a guide. Since I'm partial to pretty girls—I've already told you that—you have been selected. Shall we go?"

In my whole life I had never left October House without getting, if not exactly permission, an acknowledgment of my going. And I knew full well there were many tasks lined up for me that day. But it didn't matter to me in the least. Not wanting to stop in the weaving shed to get my bonnet, and possibly getting caught out, I threw a scarf over my head and said, "Yes, why not?" And feeling as though I were walking on air, I stepped along beside the tall, handsome man, out of the yard, across the fields, and, I was sure, into life.

2

I Talk Too Much

Darien and I had not gone very far before it became apparent to me that Amos Byers was not the only one about who liked to ask questions. But of course this was different. Mr. Byers pried into our private affairs. Darien took an interest in us. In me.

"You choose where we shall go," he said, as we left the House with its complex of outbuildings—stables, sheds, slave quarters—and started across the east meadow. "Since you have lived here all of your life, barring the first year as you told me, you must have favorite haunts that you visit frequently. I would like to see what they are."

"I don't have much time for—haunts, Mr. Richards," I said, smiling. "We're pretty busy, you know."

"They can't keep you as busy as all that! Well, then, let's go down by the river. The Oktobee, they tell me. That's where the name October House came from?"

"Yes."

"Imagination," he said, nodding. "I like that."

I was as pleased as though I myself had thought of the name. Actually it had been, they told me, Uncle Simon's mother, Jennie Browning, who had named the tavern nearly thirty years before.

"How old is your place?"

How pleasant to be asked questions one could answer! I launched into a speech about the original part having been built in the '80s, and went on, "They

added to it in 1800 and had just begun the work when
Uncle Simon's father died. His mother kept right on
with it, and ran the House until Uncle Simon was old
enough to take it over from her." I giggled a little and
said, "I think she ran it then as well," remembering
that Carolina had once told me that the reason Uncle
Simon was so long-faced much of the time was because
his mother ran October House and him too for so long
that he still resented it.

He made no comment on my humor, but said
merely, "Interesting country." His indifference stung
me. I bit my lip and resolved to be silent for a while.
"Oh," he said casually, "I think I was over this way
one day and saw an Indian mound. Could that be?"

"Probably," I replied as coldly as I could. "The
place is full of them."

"Truly?"

"Why, yes, there was once a big settlement here on
the Oktobee." I had forgotten about that silence I'd
promised myself. "Not as large as the one over to the
west, of course, where they have I guess a dozen
mounds, and they said tribes came from all over the
south to live there. That's in the Etowah Valley."

He nodded. "Yes, I've heard of it. Someday I must
go there. But where is the mound I found? I'm sure
it was here by the river."

"This way." It was a wonder that I knew. I had paid
little enough attention to the world beyond the limits
of our own tight-bordered domain. "There—there it
is."

"Yes." He strode to it and poked at the grass with
a stick he had picked up earlier. "Who knows what
might be found if one dug down deep enough."

"Skeletons," I said, making a face. "So I've been
told. There were a couple of mounds, like this but

bigger, right where the House is, you know. They found all sorts of things when they started digging for the foundations."

Actually I had very little interest in the whole subject. I had seen Uncle Simon's collection all too often. He kept it locked up in a small building behind the big stable, and I considered it ghoulish. Old bones had no interest for me, and since most of the things he set such store by were broken, I could see no good in them. Who cares about a stone ax with half a handle, or a strange-looking figure crudely carved in stone with its nose gone, or pots in all sizes and shapes and not one of them whole? Uncle Simon thought them all very important, and Carolina and I pretended interest when he deigned to show new finds to us, but neither of us cared very much.

"You must know the Indians hereabout very well," Darien said, walking around the grass-grown mound and squinting up at the top of it. I tried to resign myself. I had heard guests speak of climbing the mound, comparing its height and slope with others they had encountered as they moved around Georgia and Tennessee and the Carolinas. Uncle Simon himself came here now and again, in a rare off-moment, and I suppose he climbed the grassy hill too. I had gone upward a few yards once, but there was nothing much to see, and there were so many trees around you could scarce glimpse the river below. Well, let him climb. I would wait below, or even go up with him if it seemed to be expected of me.

The whole subject of the mounds bored me, but usually the mention of Indians made me uneasy. I was not afraid of them, you understand. It had been many years since there were any "incidents." One of William Browning's overseers and an Indian agent had been killed not long after October House was built, the first part of it, and Uncle Simon had said that although his father had kept loaded muskets at hand at all times after that, there had been no more trouble.

Actually I had seen very few Indians in my life. They traveled the roads sometimes, and more often their own faint trails, but naturally they did not stop at October House. There was one, called John, though, who appeared from nowhere every so often, disappearing again like a morning mist. He never harmed anyone, he had almost nothing to do with us at October House, and yet every time he was seen in the vicinity, things seemed to happen. Faced with it, Uncle Simon always said it was nonsense, pure imagination, mere superstition. People, he insisted, tended to forget that treaties had been signed with all the tribes long ago, and that the occasional marauding parties, detached and acting on their own, had not been seen in this century.

"Those who remained went away from here," he said calmly. "And there would be no reason for them to come back. Perhaps they were not fairly treated, and I'm afraid that may be the case, but they have left us. And yet when one appears, people see fit to take fright and to fear the worst."

In spite of that, I continued to be uneasy about John, who came and went so often. And for no reason at all. He was nothing to me, in fact I had never once heard his voice. For years I had believed him to be mute, but Carolina had assured me that he could talk when he wanted to and spoke well enough.

"Quietly, and all on one tone, so to speak," she said. "He makes no real mistakes, as you might expect, but his speech is—well, bare. Once he wanted to tell me a storm was coming and I should get under cover the bedding we were airing. He simply pointed to the sky and said, 'Rain.' And he was right. It was one of the worst storms we have ever had here."

"Perhaps he didn't know," I suggested. This had been a few years before, when I had only occasional duties to perform around the place and therefore saw little of Carolina.

"He knew. They understand these things."

At the time I had shivered, and I felt like shivering now as I thought about John. He never entered October House, except for the kitchen where he appeared now and then and was given food.

"He does not beg," Carolina said sharply, when I mentioned it. "He is our friend, and we give him food voluntarily."

"Is that the way he lives?" I asked. "Going from house to house?"

"About that I wouldn't know. When he comes here, we are pleased to feed him. Cottie has her orders."

Cottie and her family, and I suppose the other slaves, were uneasy about John too. I saw them watch him, as he walked from the kitchen to the stable or away into the forest. John was unusual, in that he had a horse, which sometimes he rode but more often left out of sight of October House. Most Indians seemed not to have horses, at least the few we saw. Why should the servants, or any of us, be afraid of John? Because he was a little different from us? Because his ancestors had fought and killed ours, just as ours had fought and killed his? I never knew, but when I saw him I invariably turned away in the other direction, and if anything odd occurred around October House at a time when he had been seen, I blamed it on John. If a pig died, it was—to me, at any rate—John's evil eye. If the mail failed to come on the stage, it was John's doing. If a milk jug was missed, John had taken it. And there was no basis for my accusations—which of course I kept to myself—because I had never heard of his causing any trouble, or of taking anything of ours.

As it happened, I had had John on my mind earlier in the day. When I had found the copper disk the day before I had thought of him, with the usual lack of reason. It looked Indian, John was an Indian, there must be a connection. And I was therefore not at all surprised when, an hour or two later, I saw John's long, lean form emerge from the thicket by the river and walk straight and silent to the kitchen. It had not occurred to me before that it was strange to accuse him of putting something into the house when I usually wished to blame him for the disappearance of something, but now, watching Darien, who was walking slowly around the base of the mound, I wondered about it anew.

I had not answered his question about knowing Indians, because he hadn't waited for an answer, but had begun his inspection of the grass-grown hill. Now he appeared on the other side and went on, as though there had been no pause in our conversation, "Do you know the Indians very well? Many live here?"

"None, that I know of," I said shortly. Indians! Really!

He looked at me sharply. "I saw one yesterday. He was unmistakable. Tall as I am, almost, and straight. One eye a little crooked."

"That must have been John," I said, as indifferently as I could. But there I was shivering again.

"John?"

"That's what people call him. I think his name is

something long and unpronounceable," I explained. I was growing weary of our talk. A discussion of John, the Indian, or of some old mound that had been made four or five hundred years before did not seem to me the most romantic conversational topic in the world. I would rather hear Darien talk about himself.

"Mr. Richards, where do you—?" I began, deciding to take matters into my own hands.

"Come, come, my name is Darien, just as yours is Phillis. Good friends don't Mr. and Miss one another, where I come from. Which, since you were about to ask me, is Virginia, originally. About this John—I own to being curious. Why does he come here? Does he sell something? How would such a man live? I wonder."

I shrugged. "I've never heard of him selling anything," I admitted. I was about to add that I'd never so much as spoken to the man when Darien said, "I suppose a bright young lady like you knows most of what goes on around here. Such as a great deal about this John, and about the Indian lore left over from the days when the Cherokees and others lived in this pleasant valley along the Oktobee River."

I tried to look knowledgeable. "As I told you before," I said modestly, "Mr. Richards—I mean, Darien—we're pretty busy at the House. I don't get out much."

"Ah, but you keep those sharp ears open, and those beautiful green eyes as well, I'm sure. Probably John sells ornaments to pretty girls like you—necklaces, eh? Bracelets? Things made of copper, or even gold? The tribes who lived here were skilled in working with both metals, I hear."

"Uncle Simon has some things of copper in his collection," I said indifferently. "Oh, that reminds me

—I found a round thing just yesterday."

"Here?" He looked around sharply, swishing at the grass with his stick.

"No. No, in the post office. I meant to ask Uncle Simon about it, but I forgot."

"In the post office? Who would put such a thing there? What did you do with it?"

"Left it there, of course."

He nodded. "Yes, of course." He looked at me thoughtfully. "I must ask your uncle to show me his collection. How fortunate that he has one. I am much interested in the work of the Indians. I should like to talk to John too."

"I imagine you won't be able to," I chuckled. "He doesn't like to talk to people. I know that much. He slinks through the woods like a wolf, and Uncle Simon says he probably doesn't even *like* people."

"One admires the Indians for that aloofness," Darien said easily. "Tell me, Phillis, are there any traces of them here? Beside mounds, I mean. Carvings on rocks, that sort of thing?"

"Not that I know of. Just the mounds." I was frankly puzzled. A glorious May afternoon, the late-spring countryside unfolding its beauty all around us, and this romantic-looking creature wanted to talk about Indians. Still, I should be content just to be here. I refused to hazard a guess as to what would happen when I returned to October House and faced the music. "Sufficient unto the day"—that was one of Uncle Simon's favorite quotations when everything was going wrong, and I had never understood it really, but it seemed appropriate at the moment.

I did desperately want to impress Darien Richards, to interest him, so I hunted about in my empty, echoing head and finally remembered something.

"Over in the mountains," I said, "there are some rocks with strange marks on them, which they say are Indian."

"Marks? What kind of marks?"

"Oh, different things. Some look like bird tracks, some are arrows, some appear to be bits of an Indian language."

"Have you seen them?" I had indeed caught his attention.

"No," I admitted. "But I know people who have. They found them quite interesting." Now, why did I say that? I wondered. For all I knew, Darien would rush over to the place where these rocks were and I'd lose him that much sooner.

"Does anyone have an idea as to their meaning?"

"No. Well, I think they sort of guess at it. I suppose if you study such things you can—well, work them out some way. Uncle Simon seems to think he can understand some of the writing on the things he has."

"This John, he wouldn't help?"

"I doubt it. I told you, he's not exactly friendly, although Uncle Simon says he is almost educated and regards him highly. Besides, there are all kinds of Indians, you know. I mean by that there are different tribes and I believe they don't speak the same language."

"That appears to be true." He nodded. "Still, we can always learn. There is one north of here who has managed to write down a Cherokee alphabet, I understand. How useful that might prove. One could learn any number of secrets."

When at last we turned back, Darien's conversation became more interesting. He told me about his boyhood home in Virginia, and that he had run away when he was but fourteen to join the army as soon as war on Great Britain was declared. While he talked, I was busy calculating his age. If he had been fourteen in June of 1812, he would be thirty now. Thirty! Well, that was not so terribly old—not at least for a man who looked as Darien did. I shifted my attention back to his words, and to the sound of his voice. He had lived as he looked, dashingly, dangerously. After the war, and he really had managed to get right into the thick of it, he had become a drifter of sorts. He had fought the Seminoles with Andrew Jackson in Florida. He had gone to work on the Cumberland Road in Maryland, before they had canceled the project during the panic in 1819. He had sailed on a coastwise ship for a year or two, going as far north as Nova Scotia, and moving about among the islands to the south. He had even lived on one of those islands for a time, as overseer on a plantation. He had been everywhere and done everything, it seemed to me, dazzled with his words and enchanted with his memories.

"But now," I said at last, as we walked to the corner of October House, "what do you do now?"

"This and that." He flashed me his brilliant smile. "I like to wander. I am one who finds himself horrified at the very thought of being tied down, of roots. Someday, I suppose—" He looked at me guardedly, and my heart did a bumping little dance for an instant. "Meantime," he went on, "I live as I like and learn as I go. It is a good life. If my horse has entirely recovered tomorrow, I will travel west of here to a town I have heard of that is called by an Indian word that means 'yellow metal.' I'm told that the yellow metal is gold, and if that's true, I'll find much to interest me. I'm sure of that."

Gold. Uncle Simon always sniffed when he heard people talk of finding gold in Georgia. He agreed that some of the artifacts found in Indian tombs were made of gold, hammered and shaped, but then, he explained, there were many foreign elements to be found in the mounds. Some of the shells, for example, were much more exotic than those picked up on the Georgia coast and must have been brought from far away. Many of the designs on pottery proved that those who worked on the jars and bowls had come from beyond the big river, the mighty Mississippi. Flint was found frequently, and flint could not be had locally. So gold too, he said, had been brought from some distance, and those who said it was native to Georgia were off the mark.

Uncle Simon made everything sound reasonable, and no doubt he was right about the gold as he was about everything else, but looking at Darien's profile as he walked along, switching his boots with the stick he still carried, I thought that if gold were to be found in our hills, this man would be the one who found it. It was easy enough to see him as one who got what he went after.

"I've heard of the place." I nodded, for indeed its name cropped up among our visitors frequently since there was an important trading post there and also, no doubt, because of the meaning of the name.

"El Dorado," Uncle Simon would mutter, giving it his own name and not its rightful one which was Dahlonega. "Everyone is looking for the pot at the end of the rainbow. The easy way to riches." And he would go back to his account books.

"And after that, where?" I ventured to ask.

Darien shrugged his wide shoulders.

"I never take more than one step at a time," he said lightly. "I can tell you one thing, though. October House will see me again before too long. I find much here to interest me, and there has been no talk of yellow metal lying in lumps on the ground!"

That quieted my anxiety. I could hardly expect him to settle down permanently, or even for any length of time, at October House, but if I were to assume it would be a regular stop for him, I could be content with that.

"I hope so," I said as evenly as I could. "We'll always be happy to see you."

" 'We'? Not just 'I,' Phillis?" he teased. "Very well, 'we' will satisfy me for now. I must go and take a look at Bolivar. Soothe him too. He is not fond of staying in his stable all day but likes to roam as I do. Thank you, Miss Phillis Randolph, for walking with me."

"Thank *you,*" I said sedately, and with a great deal of difficulty restrained myself from running the rest of the way to the House. I felt like whooping and capering. I had never been so happy. . . .

That mood, of course, could not endure for long. Carolina had wanted me, and a search had been conducted by Spice, Sugar, and their older brother, Ollie. Cottie had insisted on naming her grandsons herself, and chose names that were familiar to her in her kitchen, but her daughter Ellie, usually meek and docile, had put down her foot at the motion of calling her firstborn Oil. With Carolina's help they had finally reached the compromise of Ollie, although Cottie predictably never called the child anything but Oil. "Vinegar," Cottie had said at the time, "be such a nice name for a girl." But no girl followed, just the boy twins.

Carolina was white with anger.

"I don't know where you thought you were supposed to be," she barked, tight-lipped. "You knew we were to turn out Uncle Simon's room today." I gasped. Although this was a much-dreaded, twice-a-year chore, I had completely forgotten. "I did it by myself, with Ellie to be sure, but she is not, as you know, much help when it comes to cleaning. Too much of her mother in her. Where did you go, Miss, that no one could find you? I sent the boys out looking for you, and only two of them came back, so I lost one of them too."

It was Spice who had not returned, I decided, and I knew where Spice had gone, to the stable to croon to Bolivar, Darien's magnificent horse.

"I'm sorry, Carolina," I said as contritely as I could, and of course I *was* sorry for the extra work I had caused her. But I would not have traded the last hour or two for anything in the world. "I went for a walk."

"For a *walk!* Have you so much extra energy that you must work it off walking? I could find better ways to rid you of it. Walking! Alone?"

I had wondered what to say if I were asked that question, and in the instant of its being asked, I decided.

"No," I said with dignity. "With Darien. Darien Richards."

"Darien? Not Mr. Richards?" Carolina pushed her hair back with a dirty arm. Her face, streaked with sweat and dirt, was white and exhausted. "I see." Then she turned on her heel. "Here's Ellie. Help her put things back if you have any of that energy left," she commanded, and I heard her stumping down the stairs, slowly and stiffly, like an old woman. It was the first time she had been really angry with me and I felt badly about it, but I would not have undone the last hour even if I could, and I could not.

Ellie gave me a half-mischievous, half-frightened look, and we silently pushed the heavy four-poster

across the newly scrubbed floor, and replaced the rest
of the furniture. My remorse was growing. Carolina
had been moving those heavy pieces about in addition
to the scrubbing and polishing. And one didn't skimp
on work done in Uncle Simon's room, or anywhere
else where his eye might fall, for that matter.

As soon as we were done, I hurried away in search
of Carolina. I wanted to apologize, fully and hand-
somely, as much for the sake of my own state of mind
as for hers, I'm afraid. But she was not to be found.
Cottie, who was just starting supper, hadn't seen her.
Cottie was halfheartedly instructing Queenie, who had
been assigned to help her with the cooking, and she
banged pots about in an aggrieved manner that made
me realize Carolina had not yet made her point with
Cottie. She apparently looked upon Queenie as a re-
placement rather than an assistant. I left the charged
atmosphere of the kitchen quickly, and went looking
for Uncle Simon, but he was locked in his private office
with someone whose deep voice I didn't recognize.
Asking Ellie or Serena or Sukey would be useless. I
had found that the servants had developed a theory
that knowing nothing about anything kept them out of
trouble.

Upset, sorry about having hurt Carolina, I went out
to the weaving shed, and was just about to climb the
ladder that served as stairs to our loft, when I heard
the unmistakable sound of weeping. It was Carolina,
on her bed above, and although I wanted to comfort
her, and to apologize for any part I might have played
in her grief, I hesitated. We had never interfered with
each other, nor had we, for some reason, ever allowed
ourselves to display affection. She was entitled, I decided, to her privacy, so I went out, disconsolate and
solitary, and sat on a log at the edge of the meadow

where the branches of a large crape myrtle provided a little shade. My earlier mood of euphoria had disappeared; everything had gone wrong, somehow.

I looked around me, at a loss for amusement. I felt I couldn't just sit there and brood, and yet I was not inclined to leave the place. If Carolina should need me later, I wanted to be on hand. So, my gaze moving about idly, I chanced to look up in the trees and saw something glint in the late-afternoon sun. What, I wondered, could be caught in the cleft between branch and trunk that would shine like that? Curious, I stood up and started to cross the stretch of long grass between the trees. Suddenly I heard the hoofbeats of a horse coming rapidly in my direction. It was Bolivar, I saw immediately, rounding the corner of the stable, with Darien urging him on to great speed. Then Bolivar's leg had healed, I thought, thankful for Bolivar and for Darien, but of course my second reaction was for myself. Then he will leave tomorrow. . . .

I found I was gazing straight into the lances of the setting sun, strong and golden and taking away my sight. But there was no mistaking Bolivar and his bold thrust, nor the dashing wide-brimmed hat worn by Darien. The big black horse seemed to be galloping right at me, and although I had some notion of running back into the shelter of the tree, my feet would not move. I was frozen into a statue. But Darien wouldn't ride me down, I thought, watching with horror as the horse continued his frightening plunge. Just as I knew my end had come, and that my life was about to be stamped out by those flying, thundering hoofs, the horse swerved, and I saw Darien's hand raised high as though in benediction. I almost waved in return, until I saw he was not even looking in my direction, for the tilt of the wide brim of his hat covered his face entirely. He had raised his hand for another reason. I watched, fascinated, as he drove Bolivar straight at a tree off to my left. It was the one where I had seen something gleam just now, and as he approached it, Darien pulled Bolivar to one side, but without letting up on the pace, drove him close, almost close enough to scrape the rough bark with his gleaming black flank. As they passed it, Darien's hand went into the cleft and whatever it was that had gleamed in the sun was snatched away, taken as surely as though it had been picked off by arrow or bullet. Then Darien in his jaunty hat rode his big black horse off and out of sight. He had left October House. And he had taken with him something that glinted in the sun, something that had been hidden there for his sure hand to grasp.

I was more shaken than I could admit to anyone, or especially at this moment to myself. That Darien, who could surely have seen me clearly, would wish to ride me down I found unbearable, or even to play a prank that he must have known would frighten me badly. All our talk, all our friendship—

For the moment I had forgotten Carolina and her tears. I had troubles of my own. I went back to my perch on the log while the quivering inside me ebbed away and then I stood up, shook out my skirts, and slowly, reluctantly, carefully, walked across the field to October House. I had just turned the corner by the kitchen when I heard a voice saying, "Miss Phillis Randolph, how pleasant to see you." And I stared, unbelieving, at Darien Richards, whose bright-blue eyes were laughing at me.

3

Oktobee Falls

"B-but you—" I stammered, bewildered, "b-but you—how did you get here so quickly? I j-just saw you." I gestured back toward the meadow.

"I this very minute came from the inn," Darien said. He picked up a strand of hair that had escaped from the knot at the back of my head and tucked it in. It was a friendly gesture, and an intimate one that somehow made me blush. "I have finished packing up my gear and will leave early in the morning. Your uncle has invited me to walk over to a friend's for supper tonight, and I thought to say good-by to you now, since I will no doubt ride at first light tomorrow."

"B-but you—" I began again. "I just saw you out there, on Bolivar."

"Obviously you did not," he told me. "I have not been on Bolivar's back for two days now."

"Then someone has stolen him!" I cried. "I know it was Bolivar. He is the only black horse in the stable at the moment, and anyhow, you couldn't mistake him for another. Someone else has ridden him away."

"Bolivar does not take to being ridden by strangers," Darien said, shaking his head at me. "You have had a dream, Phillis."

In spite of myself, I shivered. A dream? A nightmare! It would be long before I'd forget the powerful black horse thudding across the meadow, headed straight for me. But Darien would know, of course, about his own horse.

"I must have," I agreed shakily.

He walked to the kitchen with me, took my hand and held it for just an instant.

"You know this isn't good-by," he said softly. "I'll be back."

"I hope so," I told him, trying to sound calm and cool. "We'll look forward to your return."

"That 'we' again," he teased me. "Very well, pretty Phillis."

I was too dazed by the look he gave me, by the "pretty Phillis"—no one had ever said that to me in my whole life—and by everything that had happened to think clearly, but later, as my cousin and I filled the trays with cold meat pies, slices of ham, steaming bowls of vegetables, and loaves of new-baked bread, I began to think about what he had said. Carolina had entered the kitchen just after I did. Her eyes were swollen, and she avoided my glance, but she said nothing and we worked together as we did every night, filling the trays for Ellie and Sukey and Serena to take upstairs to the dining hall.

Darien had said he was going with Uncle Simon to visit a friend, I thought as I worked. I had never heard of such a thing. I couldn't remember that Uncle Simon had ever been absent from a meal at October House. He was always there in his chair at the end of the long table, watching the servants and Carolina and me with sharp and critical eyes. Furthermore, except for meals he seldom mingled with the guests, never for more than a brief conversation here or there, and usually only when one of them cornered him to ask unwelcome questions. Even then he frequently thought up an excuse to get away quickly, and yet here he was, leaving us at suppertime, with a guest, and apparently taking the guest for some distance. It was all very un-Uncle-Simon-like and puzzling. He must, of course, have seen in Darien all the fine qualities that I did, must find him a cut above the others. Yes, that must be it. But where had they gone, I wondered, what "friend" were they visiting? I own I was surprised at anyone referring to an acquaintance of Uncle Simon's as a friend. I hadn't thought he had any.

Carolina must have known soon enough that Uncle Simon wasn't upstairs. One could have told something strange was afoot by the way the three serving girls acted. They giggled among themselves, they mounted the stairs more slowly, and there were no sharp messages delivered belowstairs about the meat being too thickly cut or the sauce not being warm enough. Come to think of it, I couldn't remember a meal when some words of complaint or censure had not been brought down from above. Of course Uncle Simon wasn't there!

Under other circumstances Carolina and I would have relaxed a little too, and might even have discussed this strange occasion, but there was something forbidding in her face, something cold and silent that stopped the words in my throat. I found I couldn't bring myself to apologize to her for my behavior that afternoon, not even when all the chairs had been scraped back overhead and the sound of heavy boots moving from the dining hall into the summer evening or mounting to the second-story rooms, had vanished. Not even in the silence, after all the dishes had been washed and put away, and Cottie and her daughters had left us, not even then could I find the words to speak to Carolina. So we went to bed as we had worked, silently, unhappily. Only after we had put out the candle and settled down for sleep could I go backward over the pleasant parts of my day, the walk to the mound, the good-by at the kitchen door, all of it, but when I finally went to sleep the bad moments came back to me in my dreams, a medley of thundering hoofbeats and of Carolina crying her heart out on the other bed.

Carolina must have been awake as long as I, and she also must have done considerable thinking, because when I looked at her somewhat fearfully in the morning, wondering if I was to be treated to a chill silence all day, she spoke cheerfully enough.

"I feel in my bones this is going to be one of those days when the whole world descends upon us," she said, yawning. "I believe our little spell of respite is over, and we will soon be back with too many full beds and too many empty stomachs. Three are leaving this morning, that I know. But the stage will bring the same number, no doubt, and who knows how many others will ride in from all directions."

She was chattering, for her, and I took that as a sign that she was trying valiantly to act as though nothing had happened. I was willing enough to work it out her way. I knew now what it was to have not a single friend in the world, and a few hours of that had been plenty. For all her surface friendliness, though, I had no wish to bring up the subject of Darien Richards. Perhaps I could find out by myself where he and Uncle Simon had gone. If not, I would bide my time and then question Carolina, although there was no reason why she should know if I didn't.

Carolina's dire prophecies came true. We were, in a matter of hours, almost a full house, which meant that we were two or more to a bed, the stable was crowded, Uncle Simon was distraught and bustling about answering questions and issuing orders right and left. Carolina, the servants, and I were kept at a run all day long, and it wasn't until after supper that we were able to sit down for a moment and catch our breath.

"An unusually troublesome lot," Carolina grumbled. "That Fellows man, who does he imagine himself to be? President Adams, perhaps? He must have tea brewed with his own personal tea, the brewing to be closely supervised by him. I was tempted to pour the hot water over the man's head. If he's that particular about how his tea is made, let him do it himself."

I was too tired to comment. It was unusual, though, for a guest to insist on special treatment. Our travelers seemed to have a code of their own, and since their conditions at October House were better than at most such taverns, we heard little in the way of complaint.

"I've hardly seen one of them," I said at last. "With Cottie in that mood I scarce dared leave her side."

"Good thing you didn't. She almost burned the trout at dinner, when she got so angry at poor Queenie. It will never succeed, the plan of putting Queenie in the kitchen, but we must train someone to take Cottie's place eventually. That flare-up of hers was before I went upstairs to keep an eye on things. When Cottie takes a mood, the girls seem to pick it up."

I had never heard Carolina talk so much, I thought, and I, who talked too much on occasion, could barely open my mouth!

"She burned the biscuits, you know," I said, yawning widely. "I was just a minute too late, but that was only the first batch, and there were plenty. She tried to blame it on Queenie, poor thing, who wasn't allowed near the oven!"

"One of the new ones," Carolina said, returning to

the subject of the newcomers, "reminds me of some-one. I can't imagine who. He's very young—young for being one of our guests, I mean. Perhaps his father has stopped here and they resemble each other."

"What's his name?"

"Gerald Moore, I think. Yes, Moore."

"I don't remember anyone named Moore," I said. "Oh, Carolina, I'm going to bed, early as it is. I ache, and tomorrow will be just as bad or worse."

I wanted to tell her how glad I was that we were back on speaking terms again, and perhaps she felt the same, for I caught her looking at me sidewise once or twice. Sometimes things are better left unsaid, I de-cided, as I undressed in the last of the daylight and slid thankfully into bed. No nightmares tonight, I prom-ised myself. Another night like the last one would be the death of me.

I saw Gerald Moore the next morning. He was walking about idly, speaking to two of the men who were buckling their saddlebags preparatory to leaving October House. He was, as Carolina had suggested, younger than most of our guests, and there was some-thing faintly familiar about him, although I doubted if I would have noticed if Carolina hadn't put the notion in my head. He was tall and slim and somehow grace-ful, for a man, without being in the least unmanly, I thought. His hair—and he wore no hat, which was odd —was light and ruffled, his eyes blue and, as he turned them on me, friendly. I smiled at him and trotted away to complete whatever errand I was on at the moment. There was little time for chatting, or even thinking, on days like this one.

Mr. Byers, I was happy to discover, had gone, along with Darien and fussy little Mr. Comstock. Amos By-ers had never, in the three days he had stayed with us, stopped asking questions. Carolina and I had learned to hurry away purposefully in the opposite direction whenever we saw him coming, but that didn't prevent his returning to find us later, nor his incessant querying of Cottie and the other servants. I even watched him for a few minutes out in the field, talking to the men who were spading up the new vegetable garden for Uncle Simon. He must have learned a great deal out there, I thought with a chuckle. Most strangers had trouble understanding some of the slaves, and the others wouldn't say anything on general principle. That was true, at least, of all those who had little direct contact with us and the guests in the House itself.

I couldn't imagine why Gerald Moore was here in Oktobee Falls in the first place. I had thought of him as perhaps moving his home from one part of the country to another. He didn't look to be a peddler, or old enough to be in business, since I took him to be about nineteen or twenty. It was the wrong time of year to be going to or coming from a school. But here he was, and like Mr. Byers and Darien, he appeared to like to talk to people, and he explored the neighborhood as though he hadn't a care in the world, or anything to do from one day to the next, and that in itself was a trifle suspicious.

For two days I saw him walking about, to the mound where Darien and I had been, poking around the House here and there, and once I noted Uncle Simon drawing outlines in the air to show him where the mounds had been before October House was built. Gerald came back one afternoon covered with dust, and the next morning when he returned he was soaked to the knees. Apparently, I thought—somewhat gleefully, because for no reason at all I found him a little too capable and pleasant, and delighted to see him do something foolish—apparently he had tried to ford the Oktobee and had been deceived, as most are, by its depth. On the third morning he startled me. I was folding new-laundered linen in the passageway, that being the most convenient place to do it, for some reason. It was one of the chores I happened to dislike, but although we trusted our servants and considered them honest, Carolina felt that entrusting to them a supply of good linen, or any of the dearer foodstuffs, offered too much temptation to the innocent souls who were themselves generous and perhaps expected us to be.

As I wearily sorted, folded, and smoothed, a shadow fell across my work.

"Miss Phillis Randolph?" He bowed a little stiffly. "Don't be startled, I have no psychic powers. Your uncle told me your name and also where I might find you, at this hour."

That, I thought to myself, was much more frightening than any exhibition of so-called psychic powers! Uncle Simon talking about me, and to a guest?

"He told me that he thought you might find time in the midst of your duties to show me the Falls," he said, and there was something faintly familiar about his voice. He *must* be the son of someone who has stopped with us, and more than once, I thought, for Carolina and me both to find a resemblance, faint though it was. "Here, let me." He picked up a heavy pile of linen. "Where does it go?"

"Right here." I swung open the door of the deep cupboard Uncle Simon had had built just across from his post office. It was in a way a strange place to store linen, but the passageway was more or less central, the stairway to the rooms upstairs led from it and actually slanted right over the linen cupboard, so it was convenient for several reasons.

"Here?" He slid with ease the heavy pile onto the shelf I had indicated. "Now, could we take our little journey, do you think?"

"Uncle Simon said I was to go?" I asked doubtfully. I had found myself in trouble for leaving the House only a few days before. One experience had been enough. Besides, this slender young man, although good to look at and pleasant in manner, was not Darien Richards!

"He did. I promised to bring you back before too long. I am tired of exploring by myself, and need a guide."

Suddenly everyone needs a guide, I thought. I had been to Oktobee Falls perhaps twice in my life, but I felt that I knew the way there, and as I thought about it I welcomed the chance to see them again. They were highly spoken of by everyone who had visited the spot, although our part of Georgia abounds in waterfalls of great size and beauty. Besides, my few hours of freedom earlier had taught me to enjoy the world about me, and I suddenly found that I longed for another opportunity to get away and out into the golden sunlight.

"I'll get my bonnet," I told him, since this time I had official sanction and would have relished being challenged by Carolina, for once.

When I joined Gerald several minutes later, I saw that he had a packet in his hand.

"Our dinner," he said. "We are to eat by the Falls and make a real outing of it."

It was too astonishing. Surely Uncle Simon hadn't

suggested this bit of embroidery? But no matter. Still, I thought, we should get away quickly before he, or someone, changed his mind.

"This way," I said, and we walked down to the post road, crossed it and turned north. I had a qualm or two as we moved along a forest trail. It *had* been some time since I'd visited the Falls, and I wanted not to make myself look foolish in the young man's eyes by getting us lost. He sauntered along beside me, talking almost constantly, pointing to a tree or flower, grasping my arm to hold me still, as a rabbit crossed our path or a bird flashed its bright feathers overhead. He talked well, and although his voice still troubled me—where *had* I heard it, or one like it?—I found him interesting. Nothing like Darien, of course. Gerald spoke not of sailing through hurricanes or fighting in hand-to-hand combat. Rather he told me about the islands on the coast where he came from, of the wide salt marshes where many kinds of waterfowl return each year to breed, and of the richness of the area for growing fruits and vegetables.

"I have always thought that my Sea Island was one step away from heaven," he said lightly. "But now I find that there are other places in the world with similar claims. In Georgia, even. I had heard about your mountains here, and the waterfalls and hidden lakes, but hadn't realized how weak our language sometimes is. I find it all overwhelming. I want to see *all* of it. Beginning with Oktobee Falls."

"I haven't seen the others," I told him, "but I think perhaps you *should* begin with Oktobee. Amicalola and Toccoa and many others are far larger and more impressive, I believe."

"I think the beauty of a waterfall lies not in its

height and size," he said seriously, "but in its design. And I have been told that yours is one of the handsomest."

"Yours"! I liked that. On an impulse I took off my bonnet, since we were walking under the leafy arches of trees. Patches of sun teased my face now and then, but in the green-and-gold tunnel the air was cool and pleasant. I felt carefree and happy as I walked along, swinging my old bonnet by its strings and wishing that the day could go on forever.

"Hush!" he warned sharply, and we stood listening. At first I thought it just the breeze in the trees around us, but then I knew it for the sound of the Falls, a steady far-off sound that seemed midway between a roar and a crash. "We must be close."

"Not really," I told him. "Uncle Simon says sometimes, when the air is very still or the wind is just right, we can hear the Falls at October House. I never have, but I believe him. And they're three miles apart."

We walked quickly then, and the trail became more clearly marked, as though people had come from all directions through the woods, heard that distant roar, and started toward it. Gerald now assumed the lead, and I followed him eagerly enough, anxious to see the source of the sound.

We rounded a bend in the trail, picking our way over the exposed roots that threatened to catch our feet, and, back on smooth ground again, turned our heads to the right. The first sight nearly blinded me. The late-morning sun poured all its strength on the water plunging from high above, turning each drop into a diamond, shining on every glassy surface, piercing the veil of foam in a way that somehow seemed only to intensify the light. From a silver arc of rocks, high above, the water fell in a thin glistening stream into a basin, spread itself out gracefully, and then, wide and powerful, descended in another great fall to the rock-strewn river above us. In some places the water seemed green, in others black, elsewhere silver and gold. The trees, growing tall and proud in this constantly damp atmosphere, had sparkling drops at the tip of every leaf, and edging the falling streams were pink and gray rocks, ancient and enduring.

I don't know how long we stood there in silence, trying to breathe in all the beauty before us. The sound never stopped, of course, but added to the excitement. At last Gerald sighed.

"Everything they said of it is true," he murmured. "Everything. Did you know that this is higher than the falls up in Canada called Niagara everyone speaks of, although not nearly so wide, of course? I wonder how much water tumbles down those rocks in a day. How clear the pool is below, and the stream. See, there's a way across, and I wouldn't be surprised if we could get behind the Falls if we tried."

"Behind them!" I felt that I was as close as I wanted to be to all that sound and fury. "Oh, no."

"Not if you don't want to, Phillis," he promised me. "Come, though. Someone has put those trees across the stream deliberately. It's a safe enough bridge. We can eat our dinner over there, on that rock in the shade, and—and then we'll see."

I had never eaten a meal out of doors in my life, nor alone with a young man. I suppose all of this strangeness should have affected my appetite, but if it did, it only served to increase it. I ate everything Gerald handed to me, and thought that Cottie's cold meat pies had never tasted better, nor her dark fruitcake so rich. And of course when we had finished it seemed only natural to follow Gerald along the narrow path to the

Falls and to step behind the thick curtain of water, knowing that all of that power was pouring down from right above our heads. Nor was I afraid, although I was glad enough to hold Gerald's hand tightly, while we stood there.

When we walked back into the sunlight we were almost deaf, and smiled at each other mutely until we were far enough away to be able to talk.

"It's an experience," Gerald said, shaking his head in wonder. "Don't you agree?"

"Oh, yes," I replied eagerly. "I never have—I never will—I—"

"I know." He need say nothing more.

We sat on our rock for a while, talking a little, gazing about us and staring up at the torrents falling from nearly two hundred feet, Gerald thought. We drank some of the clear cold water from our cupped hands, kneeling at the side of the stream, and Gerald made a little boat of a piece of bark and a twig, and solemnly launched it in the river.

"This," he said, "will get to October House just about the same time we do. The water runs faster than we walk, but it has a roundabout way to go, and will stop now and then to converse with a rock or branch in its path. But we'll see it."

He sounded so sure I almost believed him. And when we started walking, crossing the rough bridge of felled trees just as the little boat bobbed beneath it, I knew I didn't want to leave this place. I wanted to stay. I would come back, though, I promised myself.

At first we talked little, our minds full of what we had seen. But after a while Gerald began to question me gently, about life in October House, about Carolina and Uncle Simon, about the guests. And my mind veered away from this exciting day and, stirred as it was by what we had observed, wound itself feverishly around the memory of Darien. I thought of his black curly hair, his blue eyes, his tall and lean body. And although I tried to be polite to Gerald, I sometimes scarcely heard his questions.

"You must become acquainted with a wide variety of people," I heard him say once. "Every sort, from princes to knaves."

"I doubt we've had either at October House," I told him, laughing. "And I'm sure we've had variety, but we are too busy taking care of them to see or know them. Today," I added, "is an exception."

"Don't others ask you to show them things?" he asked. "The Falls? The Indian mounds? Things like that?"

"Not—often," I told him, thinking how odd it was that this should have happened twice within a few days.

"I found that mound by the river interesting," he said casually, "but apparently no one has ever tried to dig in it, to see what lies under the grass."

"No. You must ask Uncle Simon to show you the things they found when they dug the foundations for October House," I suggested.

"I've seen them. Very interesting. I suppose some-day they'll get around to poking into the other one."

"Why should they?" I wasn't listening, really. I was thinking about Darien swishing his stick, his wide hat shielding his face from the sun.

"Well," he began, and then stopped. "No reason, I guess. It's just that right now, with the talk of our Government sending the Cherokees away from Georgia—"

"Uncle Simon says they can't, they have no right!" I cried, having heard Uncle Simon on the subject many times lately. "What right has anyone to send them away?"

"I agree," Gerald said sadly. "I'm just mentioning what seems to be in the wind."

"I don't understand it all," I complained. "There's lots of land. Look at it! Why would anyone want to—to do such a thing?"

"Greed," he said flatly. "You know they claim to have found gold around here somewhere."

There was Darien again in my thoughts! I nodded.

"And because they find Indian things made of gold they believe the Indians found it here long ago, and if they push the tribes from their land, the gold will belong to them. It's wrong and I have no sympathy with them, but wiser heads than mine have said it could happen before too long. If Andrew Jackson is elected President this year, as seems likely since he almost achieved it four years ago, there will be short shrift for all Indian nations. He fought them for years. He's not about to be a good friend to them now."

"Oh, dear." As always, when events that had occurred, or would occur, beyond the limits of October House were discussed, I felt helpless, ignorant. "Oh, dear."

"It's wrong," Gerald said grimly. "Dead wrong. Well, perhaps it won't happen after all. But if it does, it will be a sorry time for us all, since the thieves and charlatans of the world will be beating a path to these mountains, until they find that gold does not lie about on streets, or grow on trees, or flow down the mountain streams. Let us hope something will occur to prevent their coming here at all. Your world, Miss Phillis, is much too pleasant to spoil in such a manner."

4

A Shot in the Night

My taste—two tastes, really—of freedom made me restless. I liked Gerald, but I persuaded myself that I liked the day at the Falls more than I did the young man himself. It was nice to know someone almost my own age, for a change, but Gerald was not Darien, and that of course was the trouble.

The day at the Falls would be printed on my memory forever. There had been two wrong notes struck in the great harmony of the hours which I would try to forget, but they still made me uncomfortable. Gerald's remarks about the Indians losing their rightful land depressed me. It was a subject I put away from my thoughts whenever I could, but Uncle Simon never let the matter go, worrying about it, saying in his quick, crisp voice that something must be done to stop the hotheads who were committing such folly. That he had succeeded in converting anyone as unthinking as me to his point of view was proof of his powers of persuasion, for I had always had a fear of the Indians, and wished heartily not to think of them at all. And yet on that lovely day, Gerald had brought the whole issue back from the shadowy forgetfulness to which I had tried to banish it.

The other off-key moment had been when Gerald, turning to me at a sharp curve in the trail we followed on our way back to October House, had said, "Phillis, I know you must see many people at your inn, men who come and go. But once in a while one must have a special attraction for you, a special meaning. Isn't that true?"

Darien was never out of my head, and the happy golden day had brought him close, as though we were sharing it, and I murmured, "Well, sometimes I suppose I—"

"Could you see your way clear to putting my name on the list?"

"I have no list!" I cried joyously. "But there is—"

"There is—one name then?"

I nodded and laughed happily, finding it a cause for merriment that this mere boy should think of entering his name on the same page as Darien's. Then I looked up into his face, and was surprised at the expression I saw there. He looked hurt, and just a little angry. He had concluded, I imagine, that I was laughing at him, but I was not.

The expression vanished quickly. He jumped high in the air and caught at a branch that showered us with a cascade of stored-up raindrops, and the moment passed. I hoped he would forget it, although I found I could not. I liked him very much indeed, and would never wish to hurt him. Well, he would soon forget.

Gerald stayed only two days after our excursion to the Falls. He smiled at me from a distance, spoke to me pleasantly when we met, but there were no more invitations. I saw him talking to Uncle Simon quite earnestly once or twice, and once, much to my surprise, to John. No one ever talked to John except Uncle Simon, that I had observed anyway. But there was Gerald, his light hair shining in the sun, apparently listening intently to whatever it was that John was saying, and John must be dealing in more than monosyllables. I decided I had better revise my opinion of the world around me. Things weren't quite as I had always supposed.

And then Gerald was gone. He sought me out in the kitchen, where I was somewhat hopelessly trying to persuade Cottie to clean off the chopping block before she used it for kneading her bread dough, hopelessly because I knew full well if it was to be done, I would do it, not Cottie nor Queenie, who had five minutes earlier stamped her foot and angrily marched from the kitchen. I felt, rather than saw, a shadow fall across the room, looked up and saw him there, tall and slim. It was only his outline, and I couldn't see then that he was dressed to depart, that he was smiling at me, that he had held out his hand to take mine.

"Phillis," he said in his low, deep voice, "I am leaving. I came to say good-by."

"Leaving"! It sounded so final. "Oh, I—" I began, but could think of no words. "I'm sorry to have you go," I told him finally. I wanted to thank him for the day at the Falls, for—well, everything, but the words stuck in my throat.

"I'll be back," he told me, still holding the hand that I suddenly realized was probably coated with flour, thanks to my recent tussle with Cottie. "Then we'll have another excursion together. To Oktobee Falls or elsewhere, it doesn't matter. Promise?"

I nodded, feeling childish and awkward. He gave my hand a last squeeze, turned quickly, and went away.

"Nice man?" chuckled Cottie, bobbing her head knowingly. "Nice man, Miz Phillis?"

I'm afraid I blushed. Then I turned back to the dough and the board. "Come, Cottie," I said more sharply than was necessary. "We must get on with this."

On the way back from the Falls, Gerald had questioned me at some length about the House, and because of his interrogation I had become more aware of the running of the place. Carolina had done most of it, along with Uncle Simon, while I had taken orders and done as I was bidden. Now I had begun to realize that it was a complex problem, that kitchen was linked to dining room, and the hours, even the minutes, had to be counted and assayed. When I was sent flying to one of the upper rooms to fetch this or deliver that, it was not a matter of a whim on Carolina's part, but the sure knowledge that one guest was leaving, another arriving, and all must be ready. I suppose I had known all this, but the brainwork behind each move, the motivation, had never seemed important to me. Now for the first time I realized what a mental strain it was constantly to Carolina, and to Uncle Simon, and I was ashamed that I had not thought it through before.

So for a few days I flew around as I was told to, on each occasion trying to see what was behind each order, each hurriedly barked command. And then something happened that drove all else out of my mind. Darien came back.

I had been out to the smokehouse, and was walking slowly back to the kitchen. It was late June, and after a cool week or two it had turned hot again and I felt an unfamiliar lassitude, the way one does in spring when all at once the whole world seems to bear down on your spirit. I knew I must get back to my tasks, but I had no wish to. I wanted to sink down in the tall grass and just lie there, silent and still, letting the warm golden air flow over me. Then I heard a commotion and thought wearily, More guests. More and more. We are crowded now—and automatically began to hurry, knowing that I would inevitably be needed. As

I rounded the corner I heard a hearty laugh, and I stared into the afternoon sun to see a familiar figure, tall, broad-shouldered, wearing a hat with a dashing wide brim.

Darien! In that instant I forgot I was tired, that I had lately found life dull. I picked up my skirts and ran toward him, until fortunately my head rebuked my heart, and I slowed to a more decorous pace, strolling across to the mounting block as slowly as I fancied a lady of fashion might do.

"Why, Darien," I said demurely, "how pleasant to see you again."

He grinned at me, bright-blue eyes flashing, wide mouth smiling and showing perfect white teeth.

"Miss Phillis Randolph," he said, bowing, "and how very pleasant to see you." He tossed the bridle to Spice, who had as usual at the sound of hoofbeats materialized from nowhere, and with his long, loping stride he went to the House, to see Uncle Simon and arrange for his accommodation. I felt lost and bereft, standing there. I could have been Spice, really, not the "pretty Phillis" of his earlier visit. It was an unhappy girl who went back to her dreary round of duties. How different this meeting from the last parting!

But of course the sunlight had come back into my life. No matter how he treated me, he was here and that was all that mattered. I walked back to the kitchen, and if anyone had stopped me and asked a question about anything at all, I could not have answered him. I was, by the time I reached the door, in a beautiful pink whirling haze.

By the end of the day I had regained my senses, such as they were. To help me along with the process, everything happened at once. More guests arrived, a whole stagecoachful at a time, although why suddenly everyone and his brother wanted to stop at October House I couldn't imagine. To my great displeasure, one of the new arrivals was none other than Amos Byers, whose sharp, ferretlike eyes and thin, pointed nose were again to be found everywhere, while the flat, irksome voice continued to ask questions. Carolina and I avoided him as much as we could, but he did corner me once as I was folding linen—*he* did not offer to put it away in the cupboard for me, I noticed—and this time he seemed to be fascinated by Uncle Simon's furniture. Was it made locally, who was the maker, had it been here ever since I could remember, were there secret drawers and sliding panels? that sort of thing. I told him rather rudely, I'm afraid, that I knew nothing of it, and that he should ask Uncle Simon, since if anyone knew the answers to these ridiculous questions, it would be he. He seemed not to take offense, thanked me overpolitely for my "help," and left me, to my relief. What next? I wondered. The last time we had talked he had been preoccupied with that dreary Indian mound!

We were too busy to discuss things, Carolina and I, but once when the shadow of Amos Byers crossed the kitchen door, she rolled her eyes upward and I nodded. Then we forgot him during a crisis that concerned an overturned jug of molasses, but as we prepared for bed later we had a chance to talk.

"I think it most odd that John is back here again," I said, brushing my hair vigorously, hoping to put life and sparkle in it, to capture Darien's attention and admiration. Carolina always professed to envy its glint of gold, but right now I thought it had dulled.

"Why odd?" Carolina was plaiting hers. Her hair, reddish like mine but much lighter, was thick and long, and when she finished the plait it would hang well below her waist. "He comes and goes," she added indifferently.

"Not so often as lately," I insisted. "We used to see him here for a few days, then we'd have no sight of him for a month or two. But he was here when—well, two weeks or so back, and has been here off and on ever since." "Here when Darien was," had been on my tongue, but I still thought better of discussing Darien with her.

"I believe," she said slowly, tying a strip of clean white cotton around the thick plait, "that John comes here for a purpose."

"What purpose? Cottie's food?"

"No, no, of course not. Don't forget, Phillis, John is a Cherokee, and his people lived here once. The mounds—well, although they were built long before the Cherokees came here even, at least that's what Uncle Simon says—are in a way his."

"If his people didn't build them, I don't see why," I said stubbornly.

"Well, you're right, I suppose. But John is rather alone in this world." Like me, I thought bleakly. "There is no one to help him that I can see. I fancy John's people lived here, right where October House is, once, and he comes back to see to his—well, his birthright, if you will."

I shrugged it off. It made no sense to me. I wished, though, that John would leave. He had always made me feel uncomfortable and I imagined he always would.

The very next day things began to be queer again. I found another strange object in the post office, not a copper disk this time but an irregularly shaped stone that was yellowish in color. Could this be a gold nugget? I asked myself, staring at the object in the palm of my hand. I had heard of gold nuggets but had never seen one. It was not very large, and would be of little value, I decided. But why here? The copper disk now, that had been in Mr. Quarrie's cubbyhole, I remembered—*had* been, I reminded myself, until it had been put in a tree and then snatched away by Darien, because I had completely convinced myself that was the object I had seen there. But it could not have been— I made myself stop and breathe deeply. Whenever I thought of that incident in my life I felt I was going mad. It made less sense as time went on, and I refused to think about it. Still, the copper disk had been in Mr. Quarrie's place, but this whatever-it-was I found in the Hawley girl's box, although she was now Mrs. Sterling Phillips. I seldom saw her and scarce knew Sterling by sight, but the house they had, although I had happened on it only once long ago, was a delightful place, low, rambling, yet cosy somehow, up the river. It had stuck in my mind, that house, for all these years.

But of course all of that had nothing to do with this pebble. I hesitated, put it back, took it out, put it back again. It was none of my affair, I decided. Let Uncle Simon find odd things and determine what to do with them! But in the end I stood on tiptoe and placed it on top of the honeycomb of boxes. It was not stealing, it was mislaying. I had a strange desire to see what would happen when someone appeared to look for it and not find it.

Before I had finished with the post office, there was a great deal of commotion outside. I thrust the letters in as fast as I could and hurried out to find out what was going on. Spice was there, and Old Jed and Young Jed, our stableboys. And so was Darien, and Amos Byers, and two other guests who were obviously brothers since they looked so much alike. Grimes, their name was, I thought. And everyone was shouting at everyone else, except for poor little Spice, who was cowering behind a rather old gray horse, his eyes popping with fear.

Uncle Simon, cold and calm as usual, seemed to be trying to sort some sense out of the noisy scene. It was Darien who finally succeeded in quieting everybody down.

"I see no reason for the excitement," he said flatly, "except for my own. It is my horse that is missing. And I want to know why. And if we could find out to whom this nag belongs," he added, indicating the drooping gray contemptuously, "we might have an answer."

Uncle Simon consulted quickly with Old Jed, who muttered something.

"He says the horse was 'just there,' " Uncle Simon reported to Darien.

" 'Just there'! How can a horse be 'just there'!" Darien snorted. "You mean he walked into the stable, put himself in Bolivar's box, all by himself? And politely asked Bolivar to move elsewhere, I suppose." His scorn was icy.

"It appears to have happened very much in that fashion," Uncle Simon said coldly.

"Pfaugh!" exclaimed Darien, and turned on his heel. But at that moment Sugar raced up the track from the stable to the house.

"Back. He back again!" he cried, his face beaming with excitement and pride. "Spice, you tell 'em, big black horse back!"

Uncle Simon and Darien and the others hurried away. I longed to follow, but dared not. I watched Spice as he led the gray back to the stables, trailing the others, and then stared with interest at Sugar, who had unaccountably stayed behind. Since when, I wondered, had Sugar been interested in the horses, in the stable itself? But Sugar would answer no questions, I knew that well enough, so I kept my peace. Still, I found it strange.

The next time something happened, I myself was right in the midst of it, most unhappily so. The men had had their dinner. We had one woman there that night, a pleasant-looking middle-aged female traveling with her husband and on her way to some plantation west and south of us. Women always present a problem. Occasionally, as now, a man and his wife appear, and Uncle Simon usually gives up his own room to them, unless he takes an instant dislike to the pair—or to her, at least—as sometimes happens. Uncle Simon doesn't like women very much, and if a would-be guest, overtired from riding all day, fails to look at him with the proper meekness and timid appeal, she may find herself in my bed for the night, while I creep in with Carolina. It is a crisis every time a female appears, and Carolina and I have learned to guess, at first glance, whether this new one will be put in Uncle Simon's four-poster or over the weaving shed with us. It is one of the few games we play. Fortunately Uncle Simon had liked this one on sight, so she and her husband occupied Uncle Simon's room, and Carolina and I were not disturbed. As it turned out, that was just as well.

Supper was over. Mr. and Mrs. Travers had retired to Uncle Simon's room. The men broke into little groups of two and three, as they always seemed to do, drawn together by some mutual thread—business, family, geography. One never knew. I saw the Grimes brothers together, talking earnestly, drawing little maps on an envelope. Darien was with a man we'd never seen before, a strange-appearing person with a ragged beard and tousled hair, and I heard Darien complaining that his horse had been stolen or borrowed, ridden hard, and returned. He was still very angry. "The odd thing," he said several times, "is that my horse lets no one near him but myself." He had told me that once, I recalled, and had been wrong then too. Or had he?

The girls had finished the clearing, and I was making sure that everything was put to rights in the dining hall when Uncle Simon, moving faster than I had ever seen him, hurried into the room.

"Phillis!" he barked at me. "I want you."

I had been polishing the well-worn surface of the long table with a cloth, and there was something urgent in his tone that frightened me into dropping the cloth right where it was. I hurried after him. Fire? I thought—we were always fearful of fire. Something happened to Darien? Another horse missing? Thieves —because we had heard too many tales lately of unscrupulous men who robbed inns and taverns in the dead of night. But this was not the dead of night, and in any case, Uncle Simon would not search *me* out at such a time.

I followed him to the post office, and as I looked where his finger pointed, I gasped. There was not a single white letter slanting in its box. Not one. And yet I would have sworn that except for two or three, all twenty-four had had contents earlier in the day. Not by any stretch of the imagination could Mr. Quarrie, the Hawleys and the Phillipses, the three families of Nettletons, all the others, have happened to come to the House in the last few hours. Such a thing had never once occurred.

"But, Uncle Simon!" I exclaimed. "What—where did the letters go?"

He was eyeing me sharply. Then a sort of wave of relief crossed his stern face. Distressed as I was, I could see it.

"I don't know, Phillis," he said gently, carefully. "I just wanted you to see this. I thought perhaps you might—"

I suspected he thought I had in a moment of pique or temper removed the letters myself, or perhaps had never put the mail where it belonged that morning. I decided not to embarrass him, so I said merely, "It was all here when I sorted it out this morning, Uncle Simon. Every box, or almost every one, had at least one letter in it. This can't—have—happened."

He nodded. "I agree," he said simply. "Go back to your duties. We must think on this."

I went back to the dining hall, but in my shaken state never so much as saw the cloth, and sank down on a bench to puzzle things out if I could. Why would anyone try to steal letters? I had never received one in my life, but I remembered that some years ago there had been several left in the post office for months at a time, and Uncle Simon deemed it proper to open those which had been there for too long, in an effort to find out by whom they had been written and thus to effect their return and possible delivery. The letters had been pitiful, in a way, except for those which concerned themselves with business. "Your brother is as well as can be expected." "Your mother passed away last week." "My father begs that you send some money to us—" Homely, intimate, heartbreaking messages, really, especially since they had never been received. What, I wondered, would all the letters in the world amount to?

I think our nerves were ragged. There was no explanation for the disappearance of the letters, nor of the matter of the exchange of horses. We all went about our business as best we could, but with a certain uneasiness. When things do not go forward according to custom, there are—well, problems, real or invented.

Carolina and I talked little that night as we made ourselves ready for bed. She knew, of course, of the rifling of the post office, and of the strange switching of horses. She did not know of the gold nugget, or whatever it was, or of the copper disk some time back that had appeared first in the post office and then, I had fully convinced myself, in a tree in the field. Finally, as we finished undressing we exchanged a comment or two about the newest crop of guests, murmured good night, and composed ourselves for sleep. I for one dropped off quickly. It had been a long day and an active one. So I slept and forgot everything, even the post office.

Until you have heard one, a single shot fired in the utter blackness of night means nothing. But when you are wakened from a deep and dreaming sleep, the sharp crack is frightening. And that is what happened to me that night. One moment I was sound asleep, the next I was sitting upright in my bed, quivering with fear.

"Carolina!" I gasped. "What was that?"

I saw that she too was sitting up, her arms linked around her knees, her face white in the thin moonlight.

"I—I heard a shot," I whispered. I was afraid to say it out loud. "D-didn't you?"

"Yes. Yes, of course I did." Suddenly Carolina showed the stuff she was made of. "Come, Phillis, we may be needed."

The very thought of going out into a night filled

with villains and flying bullets alarmed me, but Carolina was clearly in charge. Without further discussion we hurriedly put on our clothes and crept silently down the steep stairs to the ground. My heart was pounding wildly. Now what? I asked myself. Oh, dear, now what?

5

The Marked Rocks

"The sound came from the stable, or near it," Carolina said, frowning. "But we must get things from the kitchen. Hurry, Phillis. Please hurry."

We ran across the wet grass toward the huge dark shape of the House. The moisture dragged at my skirt and my feet slipped on the heavy dew, but I made every effort to keep up with her, trying all the while to put out of my mind the dangers to which we might be exposing ourselves. We were on some sort of fool's errand that might alter our whole lives, I thought, or even end them, and felt a shiver tingle along my spine.

Carolina rushed into the kitchen, picked up a basket, which she quickly filled with clean cloths and some vials she reached down from a top shelf, while she motioned to me to fill a pail with hot water from the kettle on the crane. We worked in silence, using the glow from the fire on the hearth as our only light. At last satisfied with the things she had collected, Carolina led me out of the kitchen and into the dark night, eerie in the pale cloud-touched moonlight. I followed her and tried not to hold back. What would happen next? More gunshots? We had heard many over the years but in the daytime, when poachers roamed our land to pick off a rabbit or two, or sometimes a deer. But in the middle of the night—that was a different kettle of fish, I thought wearily, groggy from sleep and faint with fright.

Carolina headed straight for the stable, and then waited in the dark doorway, holding out her free hand to stop and silence me. She must have heard something I did not, because she turned swiftly toward the ladder to the loft. She climbed it nimbly, then reached a hand down for the pail of hot water I clutched with aching fingers. I wanted to protest, but found no voice in my tightened throat. What had she climbed up to, or to whom? But if she was there, I must be too. I took a deep breath and slowly went up the wooden ladder toward the dim light that grew brighter as I mounted.

I suppose I knew, and Carolina did too, who we would see there. It was inevitable, in a way, that it should be Darien Richards. He was lying against a mound of hay, his shirt wrinkled and bloody, his face white but smiling. And I must have known all the time that it was Darien who had been shot when that one wild sound rang out through the silent night.

Carolina set about her task just as I knew she would. Without faltering or hesitating, she tore away the bloody shirt. The loft, the entire stable, reeled around me. I had heard of cutting bullets from wounds, using kitchen knives or whatever was handy. Could Carolina do that? Could I watch her do it? I slid down onto the slippery hay, hoping my cowardly thoughts were not reflected in my face. To my knowledge Carolina had never had a bullet wound to dress, let alone had the occasion to pry a bullet out of human flesh.

"Ah," she said, in such a low voice I could scarcely hear her. "You were not shot." The relief was obvious even in her half-whispered words. She began to bathe the wound carefully, as though she had been trained for such work. I tried not to look, but could not move my eyes away.

"No," he muttered. "Shot at, not shot."

"Then how—"

"I very foolishly thought to chase my attacker," he said, flinching as she sponged the torn skin with some strong stuff from a vial, "and I ran into a—well, a piece of loose wood, I suppose."

"Up here?"

"No. Below. I thought to hide here until daylight. Whoever it was might wish to have at me again, and I feared I couldn't go far with—with this."

Carolina nodded. She was gently applying ointment to the long jagged tear in his shoulder, and as I looked at her in the dim light of the dark lantern, I saw on her face a look of dedication that was unmistakable. This, I decided, is not just a matter of dealing with an ugly wound. It is Carolina dealing with Darien. And then I knew, and would never forget, that Darien's charm had been visible not only to me but to my cousin, who at the moment looked almost exalted.

The ordeal was over at last. Darien, grunting as he settled back against his mound of hay, smiled rather grimly and muttered his thanks to Carolina, who went about the business of cleaning up as though she performed such duties every night at this hour.

"You'll be good as new in a day or two," she told him. "But if you can manage, I think perhaps you should stay up here tonight. Jed can help you down the ladder in the morning. We'll throw you up a blanket when we get down. It grows cold at dawn. Will you stay here?"

"If you say so," he said meekly. "Thank you, doctor."

Carolina's face was whiter than ever as we went back to the kitchen, burned the bloody rags, replaced bucket and basket. She looked around to satisfy herself that there were no traces of our nocturnal adventure and we left, trudging wearily back to the beds from which we would be roused in an hour or two.

My mind was in a turmoil. It whirled with little pictures, of Carolina's face as she tended to Darien, of his courage in the face of pain, of my own helplessness at a time when I was needed.

"I wonder who shot him," I murmured, having until now been more concerned with the patient than with the cause.

"No one," she said sharply. "And don't say that again, Phillis. He has a long, deep scratch, that is all."

"Yes, Carolina," I promised meekly. But there had been a shot, and I knew that never in my life would I forget what it was like to awaken to the sharp crack that meant death or wounding. Never.

Darien walked up to the House in the morning, looking white and grim. He refused to go to his bed, but sat in a wing chair by the dining-hall fire all day, telling the curious that he had suffered a mishap in the woods and would be well in a day or two. For my part, having glimpsed Carolina's face as she tended to him, I was suddenly shy of him. I didn't know why myself. How Carolina felt about him had nothing to do with me, or did it?

The enigma of the missing mail was never explained, but the next morning I discovered that all, or most of it at least, had found its way back to the post office. I saw at once that matters were well mixed up, with two or three of the thick ones intended for Mr. Quarrie pushed into the box used by old Mrs. Nettleton, who once a month had a single thin sheet with spidery writing from her elderly sister in Atlanta. I had to take everything out of the boxes and start over. As I sorted and replaced the letters I tried to remember if any were missing. The gold nugget was, I knew that much. Although I didn't speak of that to Uncle Simon, I did report that the mail seemed to be back, and he nodded, as though he had known all the time this would happen. Perhaps he had.

Then we had another shooting. We didn't hear this one, but in the morning when Carolina and I hurried over the wet grass to the kitchen we found Amos Byers lying on the doorstep. He was conscious, but very white and obviously in pain. As though we had been trained to this sort of work, Carolina and I between us managed to get him into the kitchen and onto the table, and there she dealt with his wound which, unlike Darien's, was truly from a bullet but which, like Darien's, was superficial, although he had lost a great deal of blood. Fortunately there was no bullet to be removed, just a long fiery gash to show us the path one had taken.

"Mr. Byers," Carolina muttered as she worked, "who would shoot at you?"

"Almost anyone," he said grimly, and in spite of the pain he achieved what was almost a smile. "Almost anyone, Miss Carolina."

Carolina snorted. Yes, that is the only word for it.

"Mr. Byers," she said severely, "I would have you explain yourself, if you please. Have you so many enemies then?"

She was busy with his shoulder, dabbing away at the dried blood there, but I was simply standing by, holding cloths and such, and I looked at his face. There was a moment of blankness, then one of craft, then one of anger.

"I am not accountable to you, young lady," he said, "but I own I owe you much at the moment." I saw Carolina shoot him a direct look from her hazel eyes, which lately seemed much greener and brighter. Her square face, I thought, had somehow taken on a new —well, not beauty, but she looked more attractive than I had ever seen her. Her skin, under the freckles, had become white and transparent. Darien? my heart asked. Darien?

"It—it was—that Indian," Mr. Byers said weakly. "I'm sure of it. Yes, I'm sure. Sure."

So he wasn't sure, I thought. He was trying to persuade himself. And that was wrong, I decided, and was amazed at myself for siding with John, for once.

Carolina said nothing, but put the bandage neatly over the wound, picked up the materials we had brought with us, and quickly put them out of sight. Mr. Byers, at her suggestion, stood up with a little difficulty and, leaning on me slightly, allowed me to pilot him upstairs to where his bed was. Why, I asked myself, wasn't it Darien who was depending on me in this fashion? Why, for heaven's sake, the spindly, nosy Mr. Byers?

I suppose Carolina felt the same way. When I returned she was angrily stirring up the fire and getting things ready for breakfast. She said not a word, and I as silently pitched in to do my part. Cottie made it very clear that she had no wish to appear in the kitchen until it was time to cook, and we had long ago written off that effort. So far we had been equally unsuccessful with Queenie, who would do nothing that Cottie wouldn't do. So, daily Carolina and I stirred up the coals, boiled the water, did what must be done to ready things for her. "Sometimes I wonder," Carolina had muttered to me more than once, "which are the servants and which the owners."

She didn't say it now. She was furiously poking at the coals, making much too much fuss over them.

Taking out her temper on some inanimate object, I decided, and at the same time I made up my mind to keep out of her way. This time it had been advantageous, I realized, to have us reach the kitchen before Cottie. A wounded man, lying on the step, would have created much wild gossip in the slave quarters. As it was, Amos Byers was safely stowed away upstairs and no one the wiser, at least not if he kept his mouth shut and somehow I thought that he would.

During the day I began to tie everything in with John, the Indian, and to realize that Amos Byers had been right. John had been around October House lately more than ever before. He had been seen the day that Darien was shot at. He had been seen the day before Mr. Byers was shot. It must be John, then, I decided. It *must* be. But when I questioned Mr. Byers about it later, taking him a bowl of Cottie's nourishing thick soup, he brushed my question aside.

"No, no Indian," he said crossly. "My dear young lady, don't tell me you share in the stupid local theory of witchcraft and goodness knows what else?" He looked at me sharply. "You do not, do you?"

"Well," I floundered. "No, of course not, Mr. Byers. But John was here, and these things did happen, and you said yourself—"

"Things? What things? Well, Miss, I'm waiting."

For one moment I had a ridiculous desire to rake his wounded shoulder with my fingernails. That, I thought, would show him. But the moment passed. I would certainly not tell him about Darien.

"There was some problem a day or two ago," I said carefully, "in the post office. All of the mail disappeared. Uncle Simon was quite upset about it, let me tell you." I wished I had not started on this story. I should never have confessed to such an aberration in our post office. Uncle Simon was so proud of it. I hurried along. "But then, you see, just as mysteriously all of the letters reappeared."

"All? Are you sure all?"

Since I was not sure, I couldn't answer this question positively. "I think," I said gently, "that all of them came back. I don't," I snapped at him in a sudden burst of fury, "read the mail, you know."

Something resembling a smile touched the thin, tight lips. "I hadn't thought you did, Miss Phillis," he said courteously. "I had not for a moment thought you did."

The worry about John never really left my mind. I found myself looking for him every time I left the House, peering at trees and bushes as though I expected to see him lurking in one shadow or another. I had never liked him, but I had never before thought of him as dangerous. Now I did. First Darien, then Mr. Byers. And, I wondered dismally, who would be next? Uncle Simon? Carolina? Me?

Carolina had treated Darien's shoulder on a Monday. I had only fleeting glimpses of him on Tuesday and Wednesday, but early Thursday morning I walked around the corner of the weaving shed to see him standing there, leaning against the building. He smiled at me as though he had been waiting all day.

"Mistress Phillis," he said. "I thought if I waited here long enough, I might catch you. I have a fancy to take a ride on Bolivar, who has been pining for me and for exercise these three days. And I want you to show me the Indian rocks you told me of once before."

I gasped. Somehow every time Darien came into my life, he did things so quickly and unexpectedly I was never ready for him. I knew I must think up some excuse immeditely, so I stammered, "B-b-ut I have no horse. And b-b-besides, I am b-b-busy."

He just laughed at me. "Stop being busy, I will find you a horse, and can you think up any more excuses?"

I could indeed think of a very good one. I couldn't ride! Uncle Simon had twice put me up on the old white horse, showed me how to sit sidesaddle, led the animal around the corner of the meadow for a moment or two, and that had been the end of it. His duty done, Uncle Simon walked away from it, leaving me with the firm conviction that I would never be able to summon up enough courage to climb up on any beast again.

Yet before I knew it, I was riding a horse! Darien had borrowed a little mare from the stable.

"It belongs to that old man with the beard," he told me. "He is resting here for a few days before going on to the Coast, and is only too happy to have the horse exercised. Of course," he added, with a sly wink, "I didn't tell him his little beast will be going some forty or fifty miles before this day is done."

I gaped at him. Forty or fifty miles—that must be— why, of course—Darien had wanted to see the marked rocks, and that was where we were going. Suddenly it all seemed like great sport. And again I had no feeling of guilt. I was faced with a day of freedom, and I couldn't have been more thrilled.

"I'll be ready in a moment," I told him. I managed to push Carolina out of my mind. This was my day, and I intended to enjoy it.

Because of his wound, I suppose, and most fortunately for me, we rode slowly. At that I was quite uneasy on my precarious perch. At first I quaked at the thought that some sudden sound or motion might frighten my mount and make her go forward at a faster pace, but when after a while nothing of the kind had occurred I settled down to enjoy the novel experience. I was not too uncomfortable, and I soon got used to the slow jolting motion. It was one of those late-June days that one never forgets, blue and gold and sparkling. Although I was the native and Darien the stranger, he led me along trails and paths in the woods that I would never have even seen, by myself. Bolivar, a big horse anyway, appeared to tower over my docile little Lady Jane, but even Bolivar seemed to be content to pick his way along, with no sense of urgency. And before we knew it we were far up in the mountains.

"There," Darien said, pointing with his crop, "is in general where the marked rocks are. I saw a map, not too well done, and I recognize that bald mountain, and this deep ravine, and—well, thereabouts will be the rocks. Can you find them for us, Phillis?"

For the first time I realized that although I had admitted to Darien that I had never seen the rocks myself, I had implied that I knew people who had, and who could translate the signs and figures for us, and who would undoubtedly have told me how to find them.

"I have never seen them," I said evenly, "as I told you. But I believe that if we ride up that valley, we'll be close."

He nodded, satisfied—which is more than I was myself—and turned Bolivar toward the valley. Good fortune was attending me that morning, because before we had gone more than a hundred yards or so I heard Darien whistle. He jumped to the ground and cried out, "We're here, Phillis. Bless you. There they are."

He helped me down, and I noticed with apprehension that I was already quite sore and stiff. And we had the same distance to ride home! But I must not show my concern to Darien.

Darien tied the horses and we scrambled quite some distance up a slope to the group of large gray boulders Darien had spotted at once. When we grew close I found them disappointing. There were a dozen or so in all, and drawn into their surfaces were arrows, crude birds, symbols of some kind. I looked at them in bewilderment. Could this mark mean something? Or that one? Did the arrow point toward a mountain, perhaps, or simply into the sky? Who could possibly interpret or translate these crude and simple signs?

Darien was brushing at lichen, his face tense and sober.

"I don't understand any of it," he said at last, standing up and looking around in frustration. "Do you, Phillis? Do you know what they mean? You must."

"No, of course not. But if you're really interested," I added bravely, seeing a scowl on his face, "I could try to find out."

It seemed to satisfy him. He looked at the rocks again as though he thought to learn their secrets simply by staring at them. He was especially taken with the arrow, I saw, and walked about as though trying to find out exactly the direction of its pointing.

"Try, then," he said, nodding. "Ah, well, it has been a long ride for nothing."

"I'm glad to have seen them at last," I told him. "And it is such a lovely day."

"Yes." We went back down the slope. He helped me to mount and swung himself up on Bolivar. He was clearly disappointed. Why had he counted so much on this expedition? I had told him I didn't know the rocks, had never seen them. What difference did it make to him? They were just some old rocks that had scratches on them. Why was he so terribly curious?

On the way home I found I was tired. I tried several times to get him to talk, to tell me of his exciting life, to—well, say anything. But he answered my questions with grunts, and offered nothing in the way of information. I began to wonder if he was angry at me for having failed him.

I was also, I realized, hungry. At least Gerald Moore had thought to provide me with sustenance. But jogging along on the little mare that was now surely as tired as I was, I realized with fury that I was famished. What was the matter with this man? Then I realized that I should have thought of the food myself, and provided it. But Gerald had—oh, dear, I thought drearily, why must my mind keep returning to Gerald all of a sudden?

We had probably traveled two or three miles from the rocks when Darien pulled up Bolivar, and looked around intently.

"Ah," he said. "There is something I want to show you."

At this point I was only too glad to be helped down from Lady Jane's back, but I knew that getting up again was going to present a problem. My mind went achingly to my bed, to Cottie's food—about how just about now she would be commanding Ollie to turn the piglet on the spit—but since any delay meant spending more time with Darien, I put a good face on it. Darien led me down a path that dropped steeply into the center of the ravine, and then climbed up the other side. I knew, from the way he moved, that he had been here before. And he had not seen the rocks before?

"There," he said, with a grunt of satisfaction. He scrambled up out of a gully, pushed aside the thick branches of a wall of bushes, and beckoned me after him. He was standing, I saw with amazement, in the mouth of a cave. The opening was nearly as high as Darien was himself, and of course it was dark behind him, but I had the impression that the walls went back for some distance. Darien held out his hand.

"Come on in," he invited. "Wait till you see this place!"

It was even larger than I had imagined. The roof of it was domed, so that its greatest height was far above the high crown of Darien's hat. Along the sides were benches of sorts, made by scooping off the dirt and rock above them. A glint of sunshine revealed a hole that provided a chimney or window overhead, and its beam of light slanted to a dirt floor that was remarkably smooth and even.

"But—whose is it?" I asked, shivering, although the cave was dry and relatively warm. "Who made it?"

Darien shrugged. "Who knows?" he said indifferently. "I suppose the Indians. We are not far from the turnpike we crossed this morning. That was built because of the trade with the Cherokees, so they might have used this cave, or perhaps the traders did. Not a bad place to hide," he added, looking around thoughtfully. "Those ashes look recent to me." He crouched down and brushed at a pile of ashes with his hand. "Well, I'm not much of a woodsman. I can't really tell."

I walked over to one of the earth "benches," thought better of sitting down, and wandered around slowly.

"How did you ever find it?" I asked him. "And when?" I wanted to ask him why he hadn't mentioned it on the way north to the rocks, but thought I knew the answer to that one myself. He had been anxious to get to the rocks. But if he had been this close, had he never seen them before?

"Oh, I fell in with a couple of trappers not long ago," he said easily. "They showed it to me. They told me—"

He stopped talking and turned quickly as a shadow fell across the cave. I turned too, and saw a tall, thin figure in the opening. Instinctively I reached out a hand to Darien, but instead of taking it, he, moved away from me and toward the door.

"Who is it?" he asked sharply. "Who are you? What do you want?"

My heart was pounding wildly. I had never felt so utterly trapped in my life, standing at the back of a cave that had only one small opening, and that blocked by a menacing figure. Darien, however, advanced boldly. Perhaps men don't frighten so easily, or maybe it was just that Darien, with his long background of crises, combat, and adventure, was inured to such things. He walked slowly and carefully toward the figure which, black against the sunlit trees outside, never budged. And then he made a lunge. Hurling himself with all of his considerable strength, Darien plunged through the opening, to tackle our visitor, I supposed, and to bring him to the ground. But the figure must have sidestepped neatly, for Darien plunged beyond his target. Then, to my astonishment, Darien got to his feet and, instead of turning back to the man and to me, ran furiously through the brush.

And I—I was left with the unknown figure, who stepped back into the cave's mouth again.

"Miss," said the voice. I didn't recognize it, but I saw who it was who stood there. It was John, the Indian, and I could think of no one whose presence could strike greater fear into me at this time and in this place. "Miss," he said again. "Go to Oktobee."

He meant "we go," I found. A horse was tied next to Lady Jane, where Bolivar had been. John helped me up, mounted himself, and we rode silently. Twice he put out a hand to turn Lady Jane in another direction, onto a vague path I had not seen myself. Drooping with fatigue, I was no longer frightened of him, and I could scarcely rouse myself to look about me. Occasionally it occurred to me that he might not be taking me back to October House at all, but when I made myself look around I found a tree or stream or vista that seemed familiar. Besides, if he was leading me in the wrong direction, what could I do about it?

At last we reached the turnpike, and I knew well enough where we were.

"Thank you, John," I said carefully, "for bringing me home. I am obliged to you."

He nodded gravely, but said nothing.

"How did you find us?" I asked him.

"Follow."

"But where did Mr. Richards go? Why didn't he stay with me, with us?"

"Afraid."

I smiled at that. I could imagine Darien afraid of nothing in this world.

"John," I asked him, feeling for my words, "tell me about those rocks up there. The ones with the drawings on them. What do they mean? Can you read them?"

His dark face turned toward me, and it was darker than usual. His eyes were malevolent.

"Not for you know," he said sharply. "Not for you. No question. Stay away. Understand?"

He meant what he said. I nodded wearily as we

turned between the gateposts of October House. I would ask no more questions of him, not about the rocks or anything else. All things considered, I wished to forget the entire episode.

6

Millicent

I found that I must tell someone about my strange day. For one thing I walked so stiffly that sooner or later questions would be asked, but actually my compulsion to confess came from my inner self rather than from my physical condition. It would be unthinkable to discuss the affair with Uncle Simon. I could just see those cold gray eyes looking at me with distaste and disapproval. And, although because of Darien I would rather not have talked to Carolina about it, I knew I must. So, when we were in bed that night and the candle blown out, the night air murmuring in the trees, I told her the whole story, glad that it was dark so that she could not see my face, wishing it were not dark so I could see hers.

"I just don't understand," I finished, having taken her to the point of my sliding down from Lady Jane's back and watching John as he silently led her off to the stable. "I just don't understand what Darien was about, to go and leave me there."

"Gone for help," she said shortly.

"Help! Leaving me there alone? For all he knew John was there to kill us both, and he runs off like a rabbit and never returns."

"He probably returned with help, and was horrified to find that you had disappeared."

Carolina was trying hard to convince me that Darien's had been a normal action, but she failed. In the telling of my story I had seen the picture more clearly, and was becoming more and more sure that Darien's surprise plunge through the door of the cave was not *at* John at all, but *by* him, a calculated move to remove himself from the cave and from danger. The thought stayed like a cold hand on my heart. If what I thought was true, then Darien had committed a cowardly action. It was difficult to swallow, but I could see no other explanation for it.

Carolina, quite naturally a quiet person, has never been given to questions, and at first I was glad of it, for I had no answers. Then I began to wish she had been a little more interested in my story. I felt the need to talk of it some more. I stared into the black night, watching a star move slowly between two branches of the crape myrtle beyond the window, and moved my aching body about on the narrow bed, dreading the morning and the dreary business of getting up, of walking about with every bone and muscle protesting in pain.

Suddenly Carolina spoke.

"You need never be afraid of John," she said slowly.

"Well, I always have been. A little. But he was nice enough to me today."

"Nice enough! If you ask me, he saved your life. Could you have ridden all the way back by yourself? Found your way here?"

"No. But Darien would have come back for me, I'm sure of it."

"I'm glad you are. I'm not, not in the least."

So we had changed places in our thinking! That was the last we said that night. Her words hung in the dark air, repeating themselves again and again. In spite of my first protestations of faith in Darien, I now agreed with her. I was reluctant to admit it, but I now believed that Darien had cold-bloodedly deserted me.

My state of mind being what it was, it was no wonder I slept poorly. Every time I moved I found a new aching muscle, so that the simple act of turning over woke me again and again. It was difficult to tell, at times, whether I was awake or sleeping and dreaming. Once I heard far-off sounds that put my heart in my mouth—the noise of metal on stone, I thought, or perhaps only on sand. Someone was digging somewhere, but who would do such a stupid thing in the middle of the night?

I turned fretfully, wincing with pain, and told myself sternly that it was the nightmare memory of the cave playing tricks with my mind, and I forced myself back to my uneasy sleep. Later I woke up again, and this time I saw a light moving at some distance, but groggily turned my mind away from it, unable to trust my senses. Recently Carolina had told me that she had several times observed lights at night, but I had gaily suggested she had been dreaming. Now I tried to convince myself of the same thing.

The next morning, the first person I saw after breakfast was Darien. He caught me as I was leaving the kitchen with a basket full of kitchen linen for the laundry tubs.

"You're safe," he exclaimed. "I made sure you had returned, but nonetheless I worried about you all night long."

I peered into his face. He was telling the truth, I decided. The blue eyes were frank and clear, and there were scowling lines of worry on his forehead.

"I went back for you," he said. "It could not have been more than ten minutes later. But you were gone."

"John brought me back here," I said dully. "But where did you go? And why?"

"I had no weapon!" he said, looking surprised. "I admit that it was foolhardy of me, but I left my gun with Bolivar. I thought by taking the Indian by surprise I could get away fast enough to get to it, and have at least a fighting chance to rescue you. He would be armed, I knew that."

"I think he was not," I said quietly. "And wouldn't he have shot at you, when you ran?"

"I expected him to," he admitted wryly. "I did indeed."

"And why didn't you come back with your gun?"

"Phillis, Phillis, are you accusing me—Well, I think I can't blame you. I hadn't thought how it would look to you, but I can read your thoughts in those green eyes." He put his fist gently under my chin. "Bolivar had been untied. I had to find him. He was nearby waiting for me, but it took time. Ten minutes or so."

"I see." I could have sunk to the ground in relief. It was wonderful to believe him, to have faith in him once more.

When he left me, saying he was on his way east but would be back to October House within a month or so, I went as fast as my aching limbs would let me to find Carolina. I wanted to tell her that we had cruelly misjudged Darien, that he had been brave and not cowardly in the least. She was not where I expected to find her, checking the dining hall to make sure it was swept and clean and would be ready for the midday meal, so I walked slowly toward the sound of voices coming from Uncle Simon's office. I peered inside and saw Carolina talking earnestly to him. She was sitting on the arm of a chair, which seemed an unaccustomed pose for her, and for a moment I forgot my news as

I regarded her intently. I had remarked that my cousin had changed in the last few weeks. Her square face had become thinner, and its new lines had a kind of beauty I had never suspected in Carolina. Usually colorless, with her sandy hair and eyelashes and pale freckles, there was now a transparent look to her skin, which brightened and darkened her hazel eyes. She had said often that she was a poor copy of me, because my hair was darker and more red than hers, and my eyes green rather than hazel, but now I could see a resemblance between us that I had never caught before. She looked younger, too, and yet as she leaned toward Uncle Simon, obviously trying to persuade him of something, she looked mature and capable. I felt a great wave of affection for her, which had nothing to do with the fact that I owed her my life—my life at October House at least—or that she was my cousin, my only kin. It was affection for her, the person, Carolina Randolph, and I intended to let her know of it.

All of this took place in the blink of an eye, I suppose. I had heard not a word of what Carolina was saying, but as she finished and straightened up on her perch, Uncle Simon put his long thin fingers together steeple-fashion, in a way he has, and said, "Very well, Carolina. I will agree to do as you suggest. Unless, of course, something occurs to change my mind."

"I—thank you, Uncle Simon," Carolina said, standing up. "Oh, here's Phillis. We must tell her about it."

"About what?"

Uncle Simon looked at me thoughtfully, his gray eyes as usual boring into my soul.

"The mound," he said. "Have you visited it lately?"

"What mound?" I asked stupidly. "You mean the one down by the river? Oh, no, of course not. I went there once a while back, but—"

"How long ago?"

"Oh—" I tried to remember. Darien had been at October House in May for the first time, and it was then that he had asked me to go for a walk with him. We had gone to the mound. "Why, two months ago, maybe three," I said.

"And with whom?" he asked.

"D-darien Richards," I replied, shooting an unhappy look at Carolina. I felt she had already informed him of this, so there was little use in saying I didn't know or couldn't remember. "Why?"

"It doesn't matter," Carolina said swiftly. "Many of our guests walk down that way at one time or another, stretching their legs after riding in the coach or on their horses all day, or trying to walk off some of Cottie's good food."

Uncle Simon gave an almost imperceptible nod, but he said nothing.

"But why are you asking me this? I don't understand."

"I merely wanted to ascertain that you had not been there recently, and had seen nothing unusual. Have you?"

"No." I was still puzzled. No one had so much as mentioned the mound lately, that I could remember. Sometimes guests asked me to point out its direction, having heard of it one way or another and there being little to do in our area, but lately I could remember no one expressing interest of any kind. Gerald had talked of it, but that had been almost as long ago as my own visit to it.

"Come, Phillis, we must get to work," Carolina said, and I obediently followed her from the room.

"What's happening?" I whispered to her as we

crossed the passageway. "What is it, Carolina?"

"The mound," she said grimly, "has been dug into. Plundered, perhaps."

"Dug into? But why? Oh," I cried, "so that's what I heard!" I had to tell her all about it then. I knew she was angry with me because I hadn't spoken of it till just now, and probably also because I hadn't awakened her at the time.

"But what difference does it make?" I asked her. "We wouldn't have gone out there to see who it was, would we? And why do we care? Anyway, who would want to do such a silly thing?"

"Oh, come, Phillis," she said wearily, "you must know why. People do dig into them, to find things. Things such as Uncle Simon has in his precious collection out there. In my view, it's surprising this one wasn't tampered with long since."

"Did they find anything?"

"Phillis, are you being deliberately dense this morning? How do we know if they found anything? Uncle Simon discovered a deep cavelike hole on one side. The dirt was scattered about, but you may be sure if any gold or copper objects, or clay pots, or whatever, were pulled out, they have been removed."

"John!" I exclaimed. "John. Of course."

Carolina picked up a pile of blankets with a grunt. "These are to be washed today," she said. "It is still only August, but the nights are growing cool, and people will be calling for more covers." I nodded, suddenly remembering the kitchen linen which I had dropped right where I stood, when Darien appeared. "Phillis," she went on, "the last person to do such a thing would be John."

"Why are you so sure of that?" I asked crossly. "He's been lurking around here lately. He's an Indian. Indians built the mound and made the things in it, if there are any."

"And that's exactly why he would never disturb our mound or any other. Probably his ancestors are buried in mounds like that. The objects buried with them belong to them. He wants them left as they were. They're sacred to him, in a way. Why, when he first came here and found that October House had been built where two mounds had existed, and that Uncle Simon had put the artifacts and bones and things in that little shed of his, he became almost violent, Uncle Simon told me. With a great deal of difficulty he convinced John that October House had been built more than forty years before and that he—Uncle Simon— had nothing to do with it. He even offered, I believe, to give him his collection, to calm him down."

I giggled. "John must have been violent if Uncle Simon thought of parting with those silly things!" I exclaimed, and Carolina smiled.

"Well, he was," she agreed. "Anyway, that's the story. And we're not to tell anyone about this, Phillis. Not the guests, no one."

"Are we—is Uncle Simon going to do anything about it?"

"I have just persuaded him to tell John. If Uncle Simon tells him about the business before John discovers it for himself, then John will know we had nothing to do with it. Let him look out for the culprit," she added, shrugging, "and if he comes back, as we suppose he will, let John catch him."

I nodded. It seemed to me that John was taking up too much of our attention these days. Not long ago he was merely a shadow lurking among the trees, something to be feared a little and then forgotten. Now he appeared at unlikely moments and in unlikely places, such as a cave hitherto unknown to me, and then silently, grimly, turned into a taciturn escort to accompany me home. The anger he had showed when I mentioned the marked rocks made me believe Uncle Simon's statement that the Indian had become almost violent about the ruined mounds. Carolina must be right, I thought, when she said he probably held the mounds sacred.

Frankly, I paid little enough attention to what was going on at the moment. I was still aching, both physically and mentally, from my outing and its uncomfortable ending, but life went on at October House, and soon there came a week that promised to be one of our worst. One morning two ladies arrived on the stage, and women in October House always seemed to cause trouble not to mention a great deal of work. Uncle Simon gave up his room to these two, a heavy strong-faced widow named Mrs. Mayhew and a girl of about my own age named Millicent Graves. I loathed Millicent on sight, simply because she was the most beautiful creature I had ever seen. Her eyes were a heavenly blue, verging on the violet tones that hang above distant mountains. Her skin was clear and bright, her hair an astonishing golden-blond, with charming little curls springing out provocatively around her pretty face. Her profile was perfect, and even though she was traveling and therefore wearing sober and serviceable clothing, she looked, to my untutored eyes, as though she had just come from her dressmaker and the skillful hands of a lady's maid.

I envied her, I disliked her—and I was fascinated by her. Perhaps because of her age, I don't know, but for whatever reason on this occasion Carolina turned over the care of the female guests in Uncle Simon's room to me. Not the actual work of it, of course, but the supervision of Cress, to see that the ladies' wants were attended to. Keeping an eye on Cress simply added to my fury and frustration. Cress was sister to Job, Cottie's husband who spent his life sitting in a chair since he was paralyzed from the waist down, and there was no love lost between the sisters-in-law. Each blamed the other for Job's accident and condition, and they had by now learned to avoid each other as much as possible. Cottie had three daughters, who helped us in the kitchen and dining room. Cress had three sons, who of course worked in the fields, and Cress, a tall gaunt woman and strong as most men, often worked with them. She disliked the house, and hated being confined within it, which she made clear to Uncle Simon at all times, but when bidden she came inside and acted as lady's maid to any female travelers who stopped with us for more than a night or two. I give her credit for never showing—to them, at least—her extreme distaste at performing such service. She carried hot water, and it was always hot, she kept her eye on supplies of soap and linen, she smoothed and mended their clothes, and to my surprise in all ways served them well. When their boxes had been packed, corded, and taken downstairs, Cress vanished, and we saw her no more at the house until the next summons from Uncle Simon. It was a strange arrangement, I suppose, although I'm not sure. I have never lived anywhere else since I was old enough to observe things.

Cress liked me about as much as she liked the house, so my "supervision" consisted mostly of keeping out of her way, and that of course meant seeing as little as possible of Mrs. Mayhew and Millicent. But I had to spend some time with them, to tell them about meals and to answer questions about the mail, the schedule of the stage, October House and its surroundings. Unfortunately, women always seemed to stay with us longer than the men, who were usually anxious to get on with their work and their journeys while women, finding October House a more pleasant stop than most, often rested here for several days.

This was the case with these two. Mrs. Mayhew, for all her appearance of bulk and strength, was not well and must remain in her bed until almost noon each day, which brought about a great deal of grumbling from Cress, who of course couldn't tidy up the room until the tenants had left it. And that left Millicent at loose ends. For all her air of composure, she was shy inside, I discovered, and the very thought of going down to breakfast with the strangers who were staying at the House frightened her. I hadn't the courage to suggest that Cress carry up breakfast for either woman, and because we were very full at the time none of Cottie's daughters could be spared. So, reluctantly, I myself prepared trays and carried them up the steep stairs and from one end of October House to the other, trying from pride to keep the food warm on the journey, and yet from preference wishing it to be as unappetizing as possible so that they would decide to leave.

The second morning I did this Millicent thanked me prettily, in whispers. She gestured toward the bed, where the curtains were still drawn, and said, "I think she's still asleep. But I will—"

"Indeed I am not asleep," cried a fretful voice. "Who could sleep in this place with all the noise of voices and boots and horses and heaven knows what all stirring from the first light of day?"

Millicent shrugged lightly and smiled at me. "I'll give this to her," she said. "And thank you—Phillis, isn't it?" Those light-filled blue eyes, I thought crossly, would make a slave of anyone. I was beginning to own to myself that I had become curious about the two women. They seemed too unlike to be aunt and niece, they could not know each other too well from the questions and answers I had overheard now and again, and they were almost formally polite in their speech. Millicent, I decided, must be a paid companion, which would not be easy. I felt sorry for anyone at the beck and call of a fretful semi-invalid, and in that moment discovered that I no longer hated our pretty young guest. Even so, when I went to collect the trays, Millicent's almost untouched, Mrs. Mayhew's cleaned of every scrap, I was surprised to hear myself reply to Millicent's shy proposal that we might spend a little time together.

"I would so like to walk about, and Mrs. Mayhew is unable, you see," she said hesitantly. "I suppose you wouldn't—couldn't—" And to my astonishment I heard myself say, "I can manage an hour or so, right after dinner. Would that suit you?"

So it came about that Millicent and I walked around October House together. I told her its history, as much as I could remember, and before I knew it I was telling her my own.

"But it's like a story!" she cried delightedly. "Oh, dear, I don't mean that it hasn't been difficult for you, Phillis. But imagine being orphaned and then cared for by your cousin and your very kind uncle. It's romantic."

It did seem so, when she spoke of it. I was sorely tempted to build up my character further by telling her about my recent experience in the cave, but I didn't dare. Nor did I mention the digging in the mound. It seemed unimportant to me, although strangers might find it exciting, but I had promised. As it turned out, it was Millicent who spoke of the mound.

"That very nice gentleman who sat next to me last night at supper," she began. "Mr. Belmont, I think. He told me that you have pyramids here." I gaped at her. "Indian pyramids?" she prodded. "Or was he making sport of me?"

"Oh! Oh," I said, feeling foolish. "No, he was not. There are mounds all over Georgia, I suppose, and we have our share. I never thought of them as pyramids, you see."

"Will you show them to me?"

"I can show you one," I agreed, "but will do it tomorrow. I must go back now."

We turned about and started walking slowly back, following the edge of the clear brown Oktobee. I seldom got near the river nowadays, but I had never once approached it without wondering if Gerald's little boat, launched at the Falls, might not be bobbing gently at its edge, waiting to be recovered. I had looked today, and had caught Millicent eyeing me curiously, but she said nothing.

"Tell me about you," I said, as we strolled along under the trees. It was a perfect August day, the morning haze burned off and the breeze from the mountains fanning the air gently. I was reluctant to go back to the House, to put myself back in the business of cleaning and cooking, all the dreary work that I had lived with for so long and from which I had no escape.

"There isn't much to tell," she said. Her shyness seemed to have vanished during our hour together, and I found that I liked her more and more. I could even forgive her appearance. "Like you, I am an orphan, but have not been one for as long. I have a brother, whom I seldom see. That is not because he does not wish it, you understand, but he is very busy with—family matters. Aside from him, I have no one. No one truly related, that is."

The brother, I reflected, must be much older and obviously well off, since his sister dressed so modishly.

"But Mrs. Mayhew?" I asked. "She is not a relative?"

"Gracious no," Millicent said with a little giggle. "Do we look so much alike, Phillis?"

"Of course not," I said, laughing in spite of myself. Then it must be true, she was Mrs. Mayhew's paid companion. Perhaps Mrs. Mayhew enjoyed keeping her supplied with pretty frocks and stylish bonnets. "Who is she then?" I asked, determined to know the truth.

"She's my—well, in a sense I suppose she might be called my guardian, at least for the moment. Perhaps companion is a better term. My brother felt I should have someone with me, until I'm a little older at least. And especially when traveling, as we are now, I would require someone to be with me. She's a very nice woman," she said guardedly, "although at the moment she is feeling so poorly. That is why we have stopped here for so long. I'm glad we have, and I hope we can spend many more days, before we move on." Then she sighed. "Mrs. Mayhew is really most kind," she said reflectively. "Although I do wish she was a little more—more—"

"Human?" I suggested.

"Oh, Phillis!" The last trace of ice had been broken. We returned to October House giggling like schoolgirls, and as though we had been friends for all of our lives. She told me she was grateful for the walk and for having been shown the sights around the House, but I was the one who was grateful. For the first time in my life, I felt I had a friend of my own age.

7

River of Gold

Millicent stayed at October House for nearly two weeks, and when she left us I could have wept. I had overcome my first unreasonable jealousy, and had turned myself around in the other direction to the place where I thought her the most perfect creature in the world. That she appeared to enjoy my company enchanted me, until I realized that beside myself there was no one in or near October House as young as she, so no doubt it was a case of simply making do.

I walked down to the coach with them, and promised myself fiercely I would not cry. Mrs. Mayhew, now completely and surprisingly, I thought, recovered from her mysterious ailment, moved majestically down our slope to the stage, like a ship in full sail, and Millicent walked behind her with her head turned toward me so that I could see her blue eyes, shadowed by the becoming little cherry-red bonnet, searching my face. She looked, I decided later, as though she wanted to tell me something, but of course that could not be true. Probably her conscience troubled her, because they had decided to go on such short notice, and she wished me not to have injured feelings. Mrs. Mayhew and she were helped aboard the clumsy vehicle—this, I realized, was only the second or third time in my life I had bothered to cover the short distance through the trees to the turnpike, to view the arrival and departure of the weekly stagecoach. Millicent, sitting next to a dingy window, waved until her face was no longer visible to me, and I turned away with my heart lying like a stone in my chest. Things would be so dull now, I thought despairingly.

In that I was wrong. As usual. The very next day Darien arrived. Uncle Simon looked at him almost as though he questioned Darien's right to be here, and I confess that even I began to think his frequent stops at October House were—well, unusual. But as always, I fell instantly and completely under his spell and forgot to ask myself, much less him, why he chose to visit us so often.

The first time I spoke with him alone, I asked him, as lightly as I could, if he had ever found the town that had a name meaning "yellow metal."

"Indeed I did," he said, with a satisfied smile. "And it is a most interesting place. In fact, I plan to return there as soon as I get a few things together."

A few things. What could that mean? I began to wonder if perhaps Uncle Simon and Darien were in league somehow. Surely Uncle Simon was the only constant factor at October House, except for Carolina and me and the servants. I ticked off the guests one by one. There was no one staying with us, at the moment, who had been there at any time when Darien was, I was sure of it. So Uncle Simon, for all his chilly reception of Darien, must truly have been not only glad to see him, but expecting him. I had not forgotten that faraway evening when he had taken Darien to supper with a friend of his. Nor had I, no matter how hard I tried, discovered who the friend might be.

I was excessively glad to see Darien, although before long I saw that he had other matters on his mind but me. And, as usual, when he was with us Carolina and I became scratchy. Nothing you could put your finger on. Nothing specific. She simply barked at me more, and I retaliated by moving a thought more slowly and less willingly than usual.

On the second day of Darien's visit, Uncle Simon sent me on an unusual errand. The shed where he kept the Indian things taken from the mounds was behind the stable, and he asked me to go to it and fetch something for him. A "gorget" he called it, which he described as a round object made of shells carved somehow into an intricate design. When I asked him, blankly and reasonably enough, I thought, what a gorget might be, he said testily, "It is, or was, a protection against arrows, for the throat. But that is of no importance, it is this big around, and—well, you will know it." And with that he handed me a big key and turned back to his papers.

As I passed the stable I heard an odd mixture of giggling and wailing inside, and poked my head in to see what was going on. I was not at all surprised to see Sugar cavorting about, with Old Jed and Young Jed sitting on the bench laughing at him. We have a prison cell in the stable, you see, built when the first part of the house was, Uncle Simon told me, and stoutly, so that if a servant or highwayman or someone must be incarcerated, he could be held there until taken to a place of greater security. Spice was now inside that cell, wailing fearfully, and shaking his little fists through the strong wooden bars, while Sugar danced around on the straw-strewn floor taunting his brother. Poor Spice looked most unhappy. Frightened, even.

"Oh, come now," I remonstrated, "let the poor child out. It must be dreadful to be locked up in that place."

Old Jed looked sheepish, and barked something at Sugar, who quickly picked a key from a clutter of tools and unlocked the cell. Spice emerged so quickly I knew I had been right, the child had really been frightened.

"Don't let them have that key again," I said to Old Jed, who mumbled and nodded and disappeared into one of the horse stalls. Young Jed vanished, as did the twins. How convenient that little vanishing act must be, I thought sighing, and hurried out of the stable and toward the shed.

This little building had never been a favorite of mine. There was that bent-up skeleton in the corner for one thing, not a pretty sight. The bowls and jars, cracked or broken in pieces, the masks carved from wood into fearful faces, the rows of arrowheads, axes, fishhooks, depressed me. I found the gorget quickly, and, tucking it into my pocket, left the shed and its gruesome collection as quickly as possible.

On the way back I saw Darien. He must have spotted me at the same time, because he stepped into the shade of a tree and waited. The sun, now that it was almost September, was hot at midday, but I was surprised Darien found it warm enough to make him seek shade.

I approached him eagerly.

"Where have you been?" he asked. "I thought, by your own account, you were trapped inside the house all day and every day."

"I am sometimes sent on fool's errands," I told him. I pulled the gorget from my pocket. "See? This tremendously important object caused me to be sent away from my duties and to Uncle Simon's collection."

He took it from me, and turned it over and over in his hand.

"Shell," he said. "And yet they made such objects

of copper and even gold. Shell. Perhaps this was an earlier age."

I took it back from him. "I saw something like it once, made of copper," I said indifferently. Then I remembered. The one made of copper was the disk he had snatched from the fork in the tree, only he hadn't because there he had been by the kitchen a minute or two later. I wanted to ask him about it, but what could I ask? Did you gallop Bolivar at me, then to a tree, take a copper disk from it, and then somehow leap over the House to the kitchen door? He would think I had taken leave of my senses, and he would be right.

"Did Mr. Browning send you to get this?" he asked.

"Yes. It's a little unusual. He likes to go down and admire his treasures himself."

"Perhaps he has a buyer, someone staying at the inn who would like to purchase some of his collection."

"It's possible." I shrugged. "But I can't imagine Uncle Simon selling any of those things. He just dotes on them."

Darien laughed. "Everyone has a—a special god, I suppose," he said. "Your uncle's is his collection."

"And what is yours?" I asked boldly.

"Mine? Whatever is at hand, I suppose. Do you remember you asked me if I found the town named in the Cherokee tongue 'yellow metal'?"

"Of course." I nodded.

"At this moment that—not the town, of course, but what is there—that is my own personal god. Gold. Gold, Phillis! It runs in rivers, it lies in veins in the rocks, it is buried in the dirt for anyone who cares to dig it up. They say after a torrential rain the streets shine with it. That is a man's ultimate dream."

I had never seen him so stirred up, and I regarded

him happily. It made me feel closer to him, and I liked that. In fact, I hadn't felt this way about him since that dreadful moment in the cave when he dove past John and out into the wilderness, leaving me there alone.

"I would like to see it," I said. "Really? Gold in the rivers?"

He pointed toward the Oktobee. "Can you imagine," he said, "kneeling at the edge of that and picking up pebbles that aren't pebbles at all but nuggets of pure gold?"

"No, I can't," I said truthfully.

"Someday," he told me solemnly, "I will take you there. And you will be able to pick up a handful of nuggets, and then you will believe me."

"Oh, I believe you now," I assured him. "Of course I believe you."

Uncle Simon was waiting impatiently in his office when I delivered the gorget to him. He scarcely looked at it, but said, "You took your time, Phillis. What slowed you down, if I may ask?"

"I stopped for a moment in the stable," I said. "And then I met one of the guests on the way back."

"Which guest?"

"Mr. Richards," I said. "I showed him that—that thing. He was most interested in it." I thought that would please Uncle Simon, but instead he shook his head angrily.

"People know too much of what is going on," he barked. I left him, and I was puzzled. His statement made no sense to me, and furthermore, the small window of his office looks down toward the stable and I had for some reason the impression that he had known all along who or what had "slowed me down." I sensed he had seen us, Darien and me. But if so, why had he asked me?

I was under Darien's spell again, and much as I had been missing Millicent an hour or two before, I was now thankful she had left. Who would look at Phillis Randolph when Millicent Graves was about?

I daydreamed, then, about Darien's river of gold. I could see him leading me to the edge of the stream, pushing my hand into the clear, cold water, laughing as I brought up a handful of gold pebbles. Yet the dream made me uncomfortable. The only nugget I had ever seen in my life had been the one left in our post office, and that one had vanished. That was the time, I recalled, that the mail had also disappeared and then come back, although poked into the wrong boxes. At last this remembering led me to the fact that the coach from the west would be through the next day, and I must prepare the messages that were to go out with it.

At this time of year we were usually quite busy, until about the end of November. In December and for a month or so afterward there were few travelers, since they preferred to remain on the coastal plain, where it was warmer. To the west the mountains wore snowcaps in winter, and the ice glittered in the morning sun, but where we were for the next few weeks the nights would be chill, with the days still pleasant. The trouble with it was, as Carolina remarked to me later that day, that it was very fine here as far as climate was concerned, but there was no reason for anyone to come here and stay. No business, except for a scattering of furniture makers, no town big enough to be worth a man's time, no products, raw or finished, to buy and then to sell elsewhere.

"In other words," she said, and there was a trace of unaccustomed bitterness in her voice, "October House is, has been, and always will be, a stagecoach station. We must reconcile ourselves to that."

What did she want? I wondered. A river of gold of her own? Perhaps. Possibly we all did.

I had never discussed Millicent with Carolina, but now I felt I needed to talk about her.

"They left so suddenly," I remarked. "Millicent told me only the day before they went that she and Mrs. Mayhew planned to extend their stay another week or so, finding it so pleasant here just now. And yet the first thing I knew Cress had their boxes down there waiting for the stage, and they were gone."

Carolina and I were at the time in the springhouse, replacing the crocks we had scalded. As I talked, I saw a shadow cross the door, and to my surprise it was Uncle Simon.

"The ladies left suddenly," he said, "because of a notion the older one had. Some wish to see her son, I believe. I did not know that you speculated on our guests, Phillis, or demanded reasons for departure."

"But I didn't," I protested. "It was just—well, Millicent and I became friends. I was surprised that she left earlier than she had expected, that's all."

Uncle Simon nodded. Then he turned and walked away. His unexpected comings and goings sometimes made my flesh crawl.

"He could be an Indian," I muttered, "the way he sneaks up on us."

Carolina laughed. "You have Indians on the brain," she told me. "Which reminds me, John is back."

I groaned. Each time John left us I hoped it would be the last of him.

"And so," she went on, replacing the last clean crock with a thud, "is our friend Mr. Byers. With questions, as usual."

I groaned again. "Maybe someone will try another

shot at him," I suggested. "Do you remember when you asked him who would shoot at him, he said 'almost anyone'? I believe that!"

"There's something odd about the man," Carolina agreed. We were quiet until she said, "There, that's done. Let's go."

She went to the kitchen and I, reluctantly, to the post office. With half an eye I noted that some of the mail had been taken away. Mr. Quarrie's box was empty, and it had been full. One of the Nettletons had stopped in, because their pigeonholes were also empty, and the box reserved for outgoing post had several letters in it. One letter, addressed to Miss Millicent Graves, was tucked into the guests' box, and that surprised me, because I had not seen it before and had not put it there myself. The writing looked faintly familiar, I thought, and then shrugged it off. Handwriting is handwriting.

I put Millicent's letter into Uncle Simon's place, since he is the one who knows whether such letters should be sent on to another address, or held here for a guest's return, and as I did so I felt there was something in his box already. I reached up and pulled out a crumpled piece of paper, which was so thin that even though it was folded I could see strange marks on the inside. They looked like drawings by a backward child, I thought, and pushed the paper back into the box. Uncle Simon will jump up and down with joy at having some childish scrawl mixed up with his important mail, I thought smugly. It did not occur to me until later to wonder how the paper had come there, or when. I had sorted mail from the eastbound stage myself, and there had been no such message if it could be called by such a formal name.

Late that afternoon, Carolina told me that Darien

had left. We had an hour or so of unaccustomed idleness, and by mutual consent had gone together to the weaving shed where we sat down wordlessly. Carolina looked dreadfully tired, I thought, and I knew myself to be out of sorts. It had to do with Darien. And Millicent. And even Gerald Moore, whom we hadn't seen for some time. They were disrupting influences in my life, making me wonder why I was here, and whether I would ever be anywhere else.

On an impulse I turned to Carolina and said, "You know you have never told me, really, how I happened to come here. You were responsible, I do know that, but how did it all come about?"

It was a question I had wanted to ask her for years. How many? I don't know, three or four, perhaps, since I started to think about things. But I never seemed able to launch into it. Not that Carolina was deliberately distant with me. She just seemed to live within herself, and I had never felt capable of piercing the shell, assuring myself that in her own good time she would tell me the tale.

I leaned forward, determined to pursue it now I'd started. "Was I on your doorstep, so that you felt you must care for me? How did it happen?"

She gave me the tired smile I knew so well. It appeared when Cottie said, "Miz Carolina, we got not enough meat for today. What do I cook?" Or Uncle Simon barked, "Carolina, the weaving is behind hand again. See to it."

It was the same expression of defeat, fatigue, inability to cope. The moment I saw it I was sorry. I had never, for one moment, meant to add to her burdens. And yet I must know, and now. My sudden burning interest in my past was inexplicably linked with Darien. It was important to know who I really was, and quickly, because one day he might ask me questions. I own that her unhappy expression made me wonder if I should pursue it, though. Perhaps I would not like what I was about to hear.

"I think it's high time I told you the whole story," she said. "I've been on the brink of it many times, but I wasn't sure you cared."

Not cared! She must have seen the astonishment I felt, because she said gently, "For years I felt you weren't old enough. Later I believed in your own time you would ask. As you have now."

I nodded and waited.

"I think of it all quite often, Phillis. You see, when I was ten, I lived in a log hut with my parents, our little dog, and two very young calves we had just bought. The house was in a pleasant clearing and near a stream, and we were very happy. I know that surely. Well, one day my mother and I went out into the fields to find berries. My father—he had gone fishing, I think. We all came back at once, with my little dog, Bounce, and went in the house and my mother fixed supper for us. I remember—and this is almost all I remember clearly —that the calves, they were sweet affectionate little things just taken from their mothers, tried to push into the cabin with us. And suddenly there was a tremendous shouting outside that frightened me terribly, and then a great flash of heat and light. That's all I recall. But later they told me at that moment when the Indians sent their burning arrows at us, I had been outside the door, trying to pull one of the calves out by the tail. Therefore I escaped."

"But the Indians. Why did they—what did they want?"

"It was some roving band, bent on mischief. We had many Indians for neighbors, and they were fine friends, showing us how to plant and care for some of the crops. These were marauders, wanderers. I suppose the thatched roof—my father had not had time to replace it—I believe that tempted them. It had been terribly dry all summer, and the roof caught quickly and collapsed in flames on—on—Apparently they wanted nothing, or else they didn't see me and the calf. At any rate, they rode off, to cause more trouble elsewhere."

I shivered. "And yet you are so—so tolerant of John."

Carolina shook her head at me. "Phillis, John is a good man. And so are most of the others who come here occasionally. There were, and probably still are, some about who are—well, vicious or mischievous or both. Angry, too, because of ill-treatment. There are outlaws and highwaymen and robbers and others among our own people too, you know."

I nodded meekly, acknowledging that her little lecture had been deserved.

"Then how did you come here?" I asked, hoping to get back to the original subject, which was me.

"I never knew exactly how he did it, but in some way Uncle Simon found out about me and sent for me. I was frightened of the man who brought me here, and for a long time of Uncle Simon. And I suppose I will never get over my fear of fire."

I couldn't blame her for that. All country people, and possibly those in towns and cities as well, are afraid of fire. But to have lived through such a thing!

"And me? What about me?"

"Before I'd been here a year, someone got word to Uncle Simon that your parents had died of the fever. And knowing about you, I wanted you. I insisted. I had lost my mother and father, my little dog, my one doll, everything. I had to have something of my own. I had never stood up to Uncle Simon before—or since," she added, with a wry smile, "but I raised such a terrible tempest he sent a man to fetch you, the same one who had brought me. He died soon after."

"Oh, Carolina," I murmured, for once conscious of the ten-year-old little girl so totally bereft, instead of the one-year-old infant who was me. "I hope you've not been—sorry."

"You were mine." She smiled at me. "All mine, to raise and care for. Everything. My family. No indeed, I've never been sorry, ever."

I felt my eyes growing wet, and knew that emotion trembled in the shed. Carolina, after a moment of silence, said briskly, "I suppose Darien told you where he was going?"

"No." I was surprised. Had he told Carolina?

"He came around to the kitchen looking for Uncle Simon," Carolina said, and I could see the faint flush on her cheeks that always appeared when she spoke of Darien. "To tell him good-by. I asked him—out of mere politeness, to be sure—where he was headed, and he told me in that breezy way he has that he was going to find a river of gold." She shrugged. "How fanciful."

"He is obsessed by gold," I murmured.

"Apparently. Uncle Simon told me that there have been rumors—the men bring in new ones each week —that gold has been found in some town to the west. Not much, but enough to make everyone believe there is more if it can be searched out. I suppose Darien will be among the searchers."

"No doubt," I said as dryly as I could. It surprised me that Darien had told Carolina about it, and then wondered why I had considered myself his only confidante. It went with his dashing character, somehow, the announcement that he was off to seek his fortune, to find a river of gold.

Carolina went up to our room for something, and I sat there with my head against the frame of a dusty loom, daydreaming again. I saw Darien coming back to October House, with his hands full of gold pebbles, saying to me, "Come, Phillis, and I'll take you to the river so you can scoop up some of these for yourself." And my dream jumped to the house that Darien would build for us, on the edge of a river. Not the amber Oktobee, but a river of gold.

8

The Talking Rocks

For the first time it had struck me as a coincidence that every time Darien appeared at October House, Amos Byers followed. And the reason I noticed it this time was that, although Darien had left, Amos Byers remained. My mind roamed back over the other visits, everything that Darien did being always imprinted firmly in my head, and realized that heretofore Darien had ridden away, and shortly afterward so had Mr. Byers, just as they had arrived within hours or perhaps minutes of each other.

This time it was different. In fact, Amos Byers had been joined by two cronies, men somewhat younger than himself and most ordinary in appearance just as he was. I liked them as little as I liked him, and kept out of their way as much as possible. The Grimes brothers were still with us, and the five seemed to find much in common. I found them of little interest, but on the second day after Darien's departure, Gerald Moore rode up to our mounting block and I was surprised at how happy I was to see him. But then, I had felt deserted and sorry for myself for the last day or two.

I put down the butter crock I was carrying so hastily that it's a wonder it didn't crack, and hurried to Gerald, who was striding toward me across the brown grass. He greeted me warmly, shouted some instruction to Spice, who as usual had sprung from nowhere to lead the horse away, and steered me toward the office.

"I should have been here long ago," he told me, "and I wanted to get here sooner, but I stopped up in the mountains to look at a big tract of land being offered for sale. It was a grant of some kind that was never taken up, and is going quite cheap."

"Did you buy it?" I was impressed by anyone looking at a "tract of land" with an eye to buying it, especially anyone Gerald's age. Who was he anyway? I determined to find out something about him on this visit, if he would for once only stay here long enough.

"N-no, I didn't, but I didn't shut the door completely," he said. "I may yet. I must see your uncle, Phillis. Is he about?"

"In his office, I think." I knocked on the door, and when I heard Uncle Simon's voice I opened it. It had been my intention to go in with Gerald, thinking to learn something that way, but Gerald gently and firmly took my arm so that he could step past me and said, "Mr. Browning, I urgently wish to discuss something with you," and closed the door behind him, with me on the outside.

They were closeted there for some time. I wanted to lurk in the passageway, but was afraid Gerald would emerge suddenly and discover me there. As it was, I spent as much time as I dared at my post office, taking letters out and placing them back in the same boxes again, trying to look busy and absorbed. Finally I realized that this couldn't go on forever, so I gave it up and went to the kitchen where I belonged. When I did see Gerald, an hour or so later, he looked like a storm cloud. He and Uncle Simon must have had a violent disagreement. Over what? I didn't think they knew each other well enough to disagree about anything.

Gerald sought me out once or twice, and we talked briefly, but there were no suggestions of walking to Oktobee Falls or anywhere else. It had turned suddenly cool, and I knew that through the forest there would be trees painted in bright autumn hues—many of our guests had remarked on how early the color had started this year—and I thought wistfully of how pleasant would be a day spent in the clear air away from October House. There was something here that disturbed me, made me restless. Nothing to put a finger on. Nothing but faint suspicion. Once when I asked Carolina if she had noticed anything, she snapped at me and said she was far too busy to chase ghosts.

I was surprised one morning to see Gerald talking to Amos Byers and the two men who seemed always to be with him nowadays, Rock and Carroll their names were. I could see no connection between Amos Byers and Gerald to begin with, but that the four of them should talk together so earnestly, even going to the trouble to take paper and pencil from their pockets and scribbling away furiously now and then, truly puzzled me. At last I worked it out that Gerald was acting as agent for some wealthy man in the matter of purchasing land, and that Byers and the others might be in the same business. Only partly satisfied with this conclusion, I went about my duties.

It's a strange thing about living in the country, as far from neighbors and roads as we are, at any rate, that although we could hear wheels and hoofbeats on the turnpike, it was very rare indeed that there would be any sound from that quarter after sundown. The woods, I suppose, are dark enough anyway, and only the most foolhardy would ride through them in the pitch-black hours of night, unless he were thoroughly familiar with the road and even then he would think twice.

So our usual night noises are created by the wind in the trees, the scraping of a branch against the wooden side of the shed, the cry of a nocturnal bird or animal. We hear the chorus of crickets night after night, and become familiar with the monotonous pitch of a hoot owl. We listen, but think of other things. And then once there is a slight sound, a single note perhaps, that is just a little different. *Just* a little. And one's hair prickles on one's scalp, one's heart beats a little faster, one's ears seem to stand out from one's head.

On the first night in October, this happened to me. Carolina had been having an unusually trying time with Cottie, who declared she had the miseries and could no longer cook three meals a day nor was Queenie to be allowed in her kitchen while she was not there. Poor Carolina was exhausted and slept soundly. But I heard the—the sound. Or sounds. I couldn't tell. It was some time before I went back to sleep, and even then I slept uneasily.

In the morning everything seemed the same. Nothing had changed. I noted, though, that Uncle Simon looked as though he had spent a wakeful night, and even Gerald looked wan and tired. Something surely was afoot. The only pleasant thing about the day was that Amos Byers had left at dawn, taking Carroll and Rock with him. I thought I could face up to the hours ahead more easily if I knew I wouldn't run into that sharp nose, or find myself scrutinized by those keen, probing eyes.

The appearance of John that morning did little for my peace of mind. To my surprise, instead of going to the kitchen for food, he made straight for Uncle Simon's office. To my knowledge he had never been inside October House before, so how could he know where the office was, to begin with, and what made him think Uncle Simon would receive him there?

But he did, and they were shut up together for a long time, just as Gerald and Uncle Simon had been. My mind, running about pointlessly like a kitten chasing its tail, worried over the purpose of the conference. If I had known that Gerald was in there with them, I would have been even more concerned, but I didn't find that out until later. In the meantime I decided that the faint noises that had disturbed me the night before had to do with John. They were Indian noises, surely, signals, calls of some kind. Perhaps he had announced his coming in that way. But to whom? Uncle Simon?

Life—my life—had become a kaleidoscope, with an unseen hand turning the lens so that the bits of colored glass fell forever into new designs. Gerald left, with a hurried good-by, riding away at a tremendous pace as though his life depended on it. John vanished. Uncle Simon, on the other hand, had never been so much in evidence. It seemed to me every time I looked around I saw his tall, thin form, walking by a door, peering from a window, pacing in the field. I tried to shake off my sense of premonition. Was I going to place prosaic Uncle Simon among the many mysteries?

Less than a week later, Darien came back. Bolivar was in a sorry state, having been ridden long and hard, and Spice shook his head sadly as he led the big, tired horse to the stable. Darien too appeared to be exhausted, and I saw little of him for twenty-four hours. At the end of that time he came to me with his blue eyes shining with excitement.

"I have a plan!" he said to me, smiling at me with

that grin which would melt a flint arrowhead. "I have borrowed two horses, one for you and one for me since Bolivar is to rest another day, and you and I are going on an excursion together. Would that suit you?"

My heart lifted. At last something good was happening!

"Of course," I told him.

"I'll meet you at the stable in a half hour," he said. As soon as he'd left me I had some misgivings. I remembered how sore and lame I had been when I had gone with him before. I thought of how weary Carolina was and how I would be adding to her burden. But I also dreadfully wanted this day with Darien. I had felt dull and neglected, and now I was to spend several hours with him alone. Who knew what might come of it? I wafted a silent apology in the direction of Carolina, and made ready for the trip.

To my chagrin, I ran into Uncle Simon just as I left October House. I would have sworn that he was at that moment going over his endless accounts in his office, and yet here he was, standing by the corner of the building as though he had nothing in the world to do with his time. I felt a moment of panic. If he asked me where I was going, what on earth would I tell him? Going away for the day, with Darien Richards, on a borrowed horse? Never. Nor could I think of a lie on the spur of the moment, being unused to deceit and subterfuge. So I walked by him, trying to act natural, as though a trip to the stable was part of my regular duties and I often wore a bonnet when doing my work. To my amazement he said not a word, just turned on his heel and went back into the house.

As soon as he was out of sight, I hurried. I felt I couldn't be lucky a second time, and I had no wish to be seen by anyone else. Darien was waiting for me, and I think he caught some of my mood, because we were away immediately. His mount was most unlike Bolivar, a stringy, nervous bay, and mine was a stout matronly mare who moved like an elderly rocking horse. But the day was clear, the air still and golden, the sun high above us. And I was with Darien!

We had been on our way for only thirty minutes or so, when Darien suggested we stop by the Oktobee and let the horses drink. This in itself surprised me, and when I looked at him I thought he appeared to be listening for something. But he pulled a piece of paper from his pocket and smoothed it out. At first I didn't recognize it, but then I knew it for the folded paper I had found in Uncle Simon's box one day, the thin paper that had odd markings scratched on the inside by a heavy hand.

"Do you see this?" he asked. He handed it to me, reaching down since his horse was so much taller than mine.

I glanced at it and nodded. Symbols of some kind, I thought, or perhaps it was simply what I had first considered it, a childish scrawl.

He took it from me almost reverently. I could see his eyes were shining with some inner excitement that puzzled me. "This, my dear young lady, is to make my fortune for me. Do you see this?" He pointed to an arrow and I nodded. "Do you remember it? Well, this will point the way to my river of gold."

Remember? Had I seen that arrow before? Then I understood. Although the rocks themselves had not been sketched in, the signs and markings were those we had seen on the Indian rocks. I was excited in spite of myself.

"I thought you might like to visit the rocks again," he said genially. "And I want to see them once more myself. Furthermore, this time I know you will make them talk to me, tell me their secrets. Your uncle says you know their language."

"But I don't," I protested, "and I have never discussed them with Uncle Simon."

"Or with that Indian who hangs about? I am told he can read and write. He would know. He told you then?"

"No one told me," I said briefly. He gave me a faintly puzzled look, then smiled engagingly.

"My enigmatic little Phillis," he said. "Well, let us go along."

My mind was busy. To be sure I had tried to make him think I knew more than I did, but I had also been honest with him before, explaining that I had never seen the rocks and knew nothing of the meaning of the marks. And right now I had repeated my confession of ignorance. Yet he seemed so sure. This mental activity was slowly destroying my earlier jubilant mood, and all at once I felt as though the woods were full of eyes and ears. Behind a towering pine—was that a dark shape? The hemlocks, red oaks, chestnuts—did thin shadows slip from one to another? I found myself gazing around almost fearfully, until I scolded myself into staring straight ahead at the grass-grown trail we were following, and tried desperately to make light conversation with Darien.

Not even this went well. He answered in monosyllables, if at all. Twice he roused himself from a reverie and spoke of things he had seen since he was last at October House—a deserted village that its owners had obviously left hurriedly, because there was food on the tables, garments still hanging on pegs.

"Indians?" I asked, and my earlier fears returned with a rush. I found myself looking around again, fancying motion and sound just off our path.

"Probably," he said indifferently. "It was near one of the places where it is whispered gold has been found. The Indians nearby tried in vain to protect their land. Although the people of that village no doubt had nothing to do with it, they were routed in retaliation."

"But that's horrible!" I exclaimed. "All of it. Why are people so cruel to one another?"

Darien shrugged. "There's that gold lying there," he said lazily. "Someone must have it."

"But—" There was no use arguing with him, not today at least, in that strange mood that still frightened me slightly. We rode along in silence, and I was beginning to wish I hadn't come, and to think of poor Carolina struggling back at the House without me. In time I came to consider her not poor but lucky Carolina. The sun went behind a black cloud and gave every appearance of staying there, and the wind blowing down from Mount Enotah reminded me forcefully that we would have our first frost before many nights had gone by, and that my cloak would prove not warm enough if the sun stayed hidden for the rest of the day. There were still miles between us and those hateful rocks.

When we passed the place where Darien had tied our horses and taken me to the cave I glanced at him. His profile revealed nothing. I wondered what was going on in that handsome head, and as I looked at him a strange thing happened. I saw the sag of his chin, the crow's-feet, white in his bronzed skin, around his eyes, the mouth that was tight and grim. This was not at all the gay and pleasant young man I had seen dismounting that first day, but a man who had lived a hard and strenuous life, and who was, in a sense, wearing himself out. At that moment he turned and smiled at me, and the blue eyes caught me up in their spell yet another time. I was growing fanciful, I chided myself, and that was because of the cloud and the chill and the inescapable feeling that the forest bristled with eyes.

I was also growing tired. I pulled my old cloak as tight as I could, and for the first time wished my broad steed could go a little faster. In time, of course, we reached the bottom of the valley, and Darien turned into it and toward the rocks as though he had been here many times. And perhaps he had, I thought dully.

Darien brightened at once.

"Now we shall see," he said eagerly, and spurred his horse on. Nothing would make fat old Becky hurry, so we plodded along after him. He waited until I slid down, tied Becky beside his horse, and rushed away without a word. He was standing in front of the boulders when I had climbed up to him, the paper in his hand.

"Now," he said, "you will tell me all the secrets of the place. The arrow—does it point to the gold? It must, for all it seems to launch itself into the air. Perhaps if one figured out a trajectory for it—if one loosed an arrow on this spot, in that precise direction, for example—where would it fall?"

He looked at me expectantly, and for some reason I felt afraid. He was much too taut, too intense. He truly expected an answer from me, an answer that had meaning and that would produce results, and I had none.

"Darien," I said helplessly, "I have not the faintest idea of what any of this means."

"Oh? I suppose you have never seen this paper before?"

"No. Well, yes, but—"

He stepped close to me. I could feel the warmth of his body, his breath on my face, the power of those blazing blue eyes.

"Phillis, don't play games with me. I am not a child. I will know what these rocks say, and I will know now. They will talk as though they had voices, except the voice will be your voice. *Now!*"

Then I was frightened. The tall man at my side was capable of anything, I felt sure, and he stood within inches of me, threatening me in some unspoken way. If only, I thought, my mind scurrying about in fear, I could manufacture some meaning for those rocks, then I could get away. I could find my own road back to October House this time. And I would. My fear turned to a desire for action, any action, and without thinking of it or of the consequences of my movement, I turned away from him, picking up my heavy skirts and running as fast as I could down toward the horses.

If I had had my wits about me, I would have known how foolishly I was behaving. His long legs brought him to me in an instant. Encumbered as I was by heavy skirts and long cloak, I hadn't a chance of getting away from him. He seized me by the arms and whirled me around with such violence that my bonnet fell back and my hair tumbled loosely down. I looked up into the eyes that were still blue and bright, but right now almost as cold as ice, and I saw hatred in them, and fury.

"Let—let me go," I said weakly.

"Not until you tell me what I must know."

He was a madman in his greed. I could see it inescapably. I looked around wildly. Was I to die right here, in front of marked boulders strewn around on the slope of the valley, within sight of the naked rocky dome of Mount Enotah? What a strange ending to a

life that had been lived, except for its first year, within
a few rods of an inn, a life of drudgery and ever
lacking in excitement. . . .

All of this flashed through my addled brain as I felt
the grip on my arms tighten until I cried out in pain.

"L-let me go," I said again hopelessly.

"Not until you tell me what I have asked you to tell
me."

"Let her go." We both turned in surprise. We had
been two people alone in the world, but here was
another voice and we were three.

"Gerald!" I heard a thin voice cry his name, and
had no idea at the time that it was mine. It was Gerald,
on a big black horse, and he had a gun. Gerald, with
a gun?

"John," called Gerald, without taking his eyes from
Darien. "Amos."

Now there was a crowd of them. Amos Byers,
Rock, Carroll, John, and Gerald. Amos Byers and one
of his friends started toward Darien, who had let go
of my arms and was just standing there, tight as a
spring. And, just as he had before, he launched himself
into a headlong flight, although this time instead of
plunging through the mouth of a cave he sped like an
arrow down into the ravine and up the other side. I
cringed, expecting a shot from Gerald's gun, but there
was no sound other than the crashing and pounding of
Darien's flight.

"I know how you feel, Byers," Gerald said, looking
down at Amos Byers' grim face, "but this is not the
time or the place, and you know it. You now have
what you need, I imagine, and since you also have his
favorite horse back in the stable there's a good chance
he'll return to October House for him."

I could only stare and shake my head. I didn't understand anything that was going on. I couldn't see why Gerald should have come here, and that the others were with him made it even stranger to me.

"I don't understand," I said at last. "Why, Gerald, that horse looks like Bolivar. But he isn't, is he?"

"This is Paladin, Bolivar's brother," he said. "Come on up on his back with me. The boys will take yours home."

We rode in silence through the forests, which no longer had eyes and ears, but looked safe and comfortable. Gerald had put me in front of him, so that his arms were around me, and the fears of the last hour or two were slowly leaving me.

"I don't understand anything," I said at last, after trying futilely to make some sense of what had happened.

"It's a long story, Phillis, but I'll make a beginning on it," he told me. "Wait till I put my thoughts in order. It's been quite a day."

"First of all, why did you come here?"

"To get you, of course."

"But how did you know I'd be here? Back there, I mean."

"It was—well, planned, in a way. Your uncle let Darien see the message he was looking at just now. On purpose."

"Uncle Simon? But why?"

"To get him to come up here."

"But why?"

Gerald sighed. "Darien has some papers that he never allows to leave him, and with good reason. They are stolen papers, for the most part, deeds for land, that sort of thing. And, we strongly suspect, a few others he has forged, to give himself ownership of acres he deems valuable. Acres presumed to have gold under them, principally. We thought if he came up here with you, he wouldn't bother to take the packet with him, and he would think himself safe enough up here anyway."

"But why—why—I mean, how did you know I'd be with him?"

"You, my poor Phillis," he said grimly, "were being used as bait."

"Bait!"

"Your uncle—and I nearly killed him with my bare hands for this—told Darien that you knew the meaning of the markings on the rocks. He told him you would make the rocks talk for him, tell him where to find the fortune he's after. Darien could never resist such bait as that, even though he has become most careful with his property lately, sleeping with it under his pillow, taking it to meals, never letting it out of his hands—as Amos Byers found out, to his cost."

"His cost? What do you mean?"

"Amos told me that you and Carolina had very kindly and efficiently dressed his wound. Well, he—"

I tried to turn so that I could see Gerald's face, but couldn't manage. "Did—did Darien shoot him?"

"Shot *at* him," he corrected me. "I feel it's safe to say he's not a killer—yet, anyway. Probably Darien suspected that he was being watched, so he laid a trap, making a great show of packing his saddlebags and carrying them to the stable, announcing he would leave before daylight. Thinking, I suppose, to make Amos lose balance by hurrying. Darien was presumably sleeping in his bed, but Amos did what he was supposed to do, and went down to the stable where Darien was waiting. He's a good shot, Darien is, and he had Amos at close range, so we are fairly sure he meant only to warn him, but Amos, by his own account, all but jumped into the path of the bullet at the wrong moment."

"But, Darien—who shot him? Or tried to?"

"I'd forgotten you knew about that. It was one of John's men, and it was, John assured us and we believe him, an accident. John was much disturbed about it, because what he does *not* want is any show of violence on the part of the Indians who are merely trying to save their land and above all be peaceable. Somehow the shot seems to have frightened Darien into damaging himself in a most peculiar accident. Loose board in a well-kept stable? It's very unlikely."

I had never given the matter any thought, but I could see the truth in Gerald's remark. The stable was always in fine condition. Uncle Simon insisted on it.

"What does Mr. Byers have to do with it anyway?" I asked.

"He works for the Federal Government," Gerald said. "That's all I can tell you now. A serious charge of intended fraud is involved."

I sighed. Things were too mixed up for me. Finally I twisted around so I could look into Gerald's face.

"And you? Do you work for the Federal Government too?"

"No, indeed."

"Then why," I asked hesitantly, "are you—here? Mixed up in this? What is it all to you?"

"That's very simple, Phillis," he said gently. "Darien Richards is my uncle, my father's younger brother. My name is really Gerald Richards. I took the Moore to throw Darien off the scent if our paths should ever cross, which they have only when I intended that they should. I've been pursuing my gallant uncle for two years almost."

"But why?"

"Darien's first bit of skulduggery was stealing from my father. A little money, some objects of worth, but mostly land. Our deeds are among those I spoke of before. Before my father died he asked me to find his younger brother and bring him to justice. Frankly, I hadn't intended to go that far, but I did plan to get back what was ours. Then I discovered that his first act of villainy had apparently been so successful that Darien had decided to make a career of it, and consequently he had committed so many other crimes, large and small, that I decided he must be dealt with. I also found there were others after him. It's been quite an eventful period," he confessed with a smile. "I wouldn't want to go through it another time. But I'll tell you the rest after we get you back to October House, and rested."

I turned back to a more comfortable position. As I looked at the horse's black ears in front of me, for some reason I thought of the time I had believed Darien had tried to ride me down on Bolivar, and had then seen him around the corner of the house.

"It was you," I murmured, "snatching that—that thing from the tree. On Paladin."

"No, indeed, I have never had Paladin anywhere near me when my uncle was hard by. He would know I was there if he saw him. Paladin's been kept well away, until now."

"Then it wasn't you?"

"It was. But on Bolivar."

"But Darien said Bolivar wouldn't let anyone else ride him."

"He won't," Gerald said grimly. "Just Darien and me. You see, Bolivar is one of the things Darien stole from us. He's mine."

9

Part of the Story

Gerald chose to follow the river for the last mile or so, and we therefore approached the stable from the rear. This suited me, and I hoped I could slip through the meadow to the weaving shed without being seen, since at the moment I felt most unequal to answering questions. I was also building up considerable resentment within myself over Gerald's statement that Uncle Simon had proposed me for "bait." I knew he cared nothing for me and had long been resigned to it, but this seemed to go beyond mere dislike. When I was less tired and confused, I thought, I would think it through and decide what to do with myself. I couldn't live under the same roof with a man who had willingly, purposely even, exposed me to danger.

As we pulled up before the stable door, hands reached up to help me down from Paladin. I assumed it was Old Jed and didn't give him a glance. But when I was on the ground, rocking with fatigue and nerves, I suppose, I felt myself clasped in the arms that had assisted me. I glanced up in amazement, and saw Uncle Simon's troubled face.

"My dear child," he said, holding me close. "My dear child."

It was the first time Uncle Simon had touched me with anything like affection that I knew of. Certainly the first time he had ever spoken words of endearment to me. I was struck mute and could only stare at him.

"I am so happy to see you back," he murmured. "And relieved. Gerald, you were quite right, we should not have allowed her to suffer such risks. I blame myself completely."

"It's all right, Uncle Simon," I said, finding my voice at last. "Here I am, you see, safe and sound."

"There was no danger," Gerald said, nodding. "You were right about that. With all of us there to watch and guard her."

Uncle Simon released me, and said ruefully, "I will never forgive myself for this. Run along, Phillis. You are tired and would like to clean up. Now, Gerald, about the rest of the affair, I think . . ."

I smiled to myself as I trudged wearily to the weaving shed. His welcome had been genuinely warm, he had been truly disturbed, I knew that. And yet when he dismissed me he was able to turn away from me completely, forgetting my existence in the blink of an eye in the press of his business.

In the room over the looms I took off my cloak and my soiled and crumpled dress, washed my face and combed my tangled hair, and then, almost without knowing what I did, dropped on my bed and went immediately off into a deep sleep. I slept for nearly an hour, dreamlessly, but it seemed to me when I awoke it was to a nightmare. The memory of Darien plunging away through the brush was blurred and grotesque. Gerald's words mocked me. The long ride back on Paladin was unreal, and was part of the confusion until I remembered Gerald's arms around me. Then I thought of Uncle Simon's concern, and brightened. It was not entirely a nightmare after all, and who knew what might lie just around the corner? I got up quickly, dressed, and went to the kitchen.

"Uncle Simon wants you," Carolina said, turning

from her work of loading trays with cutlery, mugs, and bowls, to be carried up for supper. "Are you all right, Phillis?"

I nodded. "Fine," I said, wondering how much she knew but judging from her wan face and unhappy expression that she had been told about Darien. I hurried to the other end of the house. The door to Uncle Simon's office was open, and he was waiting for me, for he said at once, "Come in, Phillis. Close the door if you will."

I looked around. Gerald was there, and although well over an hour had passed since we arrived on Paladin, he was still travel-stained. He looked at me anxiously and smiled when he saw I was quite obviously none the worse for my experience. On the other side of Uncle Simon's desk sat Amos Byers and one of the men—Carroll, I thought.

"Phillis, we must ask you some questions," Uncle Simon began. "Things didn't work out quite as planned. Sit down, sit down," he added hastily, sounding more like himself. "Now, Amos, will you start?"

Amos Byers smiled at me. I had never liked the man and never would, I thought, but when he smiled his face was less like that of a weasel. I must have been a little light-headed, because in spite of the solemnity I saw all around me I wanted to giggle and say, "No one can ask questions as well as Mr. Byers." But I composed my face to look suitably grave, and gazed at him respectfully.

"Miss Phillis," he said, "Mr.—er, Moore, has told you of our plan. We thought—no, let me go back a bit. Mr. Richards has a pouch of valuable papers, among other things, that he is very careful to keep with him at all times. Our first thought was to encourage him to go to the Indian rocks, by giving him a key, however false, that he might expect would unlock their secrets for him. John had told us that because of the terrain his horse must be left many yards below the rocks and actually out of sight for a person examining them. We hoped he would leave his pouch in the saddlebag. But as Mr. Browning pointed out"—I looked at Uncle Simon, who shook his head as though acknowledging his mistake—"there would be no reason for him not to carry the pouch with him. Instinct alone would make him take it, to say nothing of habit, so we devised a scheme that we thought might make him leave the pouch behind. Mr. Browning felt that it would, and we agreed with him, although Mr. Richards fought us to the end." I saw with surprise that he was motioning with his head toward Gerald. And then I remembered that he *was* Mr. Richards.

"We decided," Mr. Byers went on, "that if the elder Mr. Richards had a pretty girl at his side, he would weigh the scant possibility that someone might find the pouch secreted in his saddlebag against the very real fact of looking a little ridiculous in front of his companion. We knew, of course, that he might have some story all ready for such a contingency, some glib reply should you be curious about why he carried with him a useless-looking leather pouch. But we decided to risk it."

"And you, Phillis," Uncle Simon said gravely.

"Please, Uncle Simon. I'm here, I'm all right. Don't think of it now." Then I turned to Mr. Byers. "It worked, didn't it? He had nothing in his hands except that piece of paper. Oh!" I exclaimed suddenly, "you made that yourself, didn't you, Uncle Simon, and put it in your own box?"

"No," Uncle Simon said. "John did it. At our suggestions, of course. And put it in the box. The right box this time," he added. "Do you remember the day the mail disappeared? I knew John had left something for me—"

"Gold? A gold nugget?"

"Why, yes, how did you know?"

"I found it," I admitted. "I didn't know what to do with it so I put it on top of the boxes, and then it disappeared."

"Darien, doubtless," said Gerald, speaking for the first time. "Anything that smells of gold Darien can find!"

"But what about the letters? Did he take them too?"

Uncle Simon chuckled, a most unexpected sound coming from him, but it was Amos Byers who answered me.

"*I* took them, Miss Phillis," he said. "This was before your uncle managed to explain to John that there was supposed to be some sort of order in the post office. He took everything out and dumped it on the table. He was looking for the nugget, and the fact that the letters were in separate compartments meant nothing to him."

He stopped for breath, and I found myself wondering why John had put a gold nugget in a box, and then wanted to take it out again, but decided it didn't make much difference. However, my perplexity must have shown, because Uncle Simon sighed and said, "We had better tell her about that too, Amos. She might know something useful. You see," he went on, turning to me, "putting strange objects in the boxes was John's idea. Actually the gold nugget was a simple signal to let us know that Mr. Richards had been looking for gold, had found some, and was coming back to October House."

"That—that pebble told you all that?"

Uncle Simon laughed. "John meant it to tell us that, and I suppose in effect it did."

"But why did he want it back then? How would he know you had seen it?"

"It would have been moved from one box to another. John's signals, as you see, are inherently simple. But you moved it a little too far, because later he came to me in some distress, asking me what I had done with it."

"Is he interested in gold too?"

"No, he wanted to return it to Mr. Richards' cache of stolen objects. I suppose he reasoned if things started to disappear and the loss was noticed, Mr. Richards would be more difficult to catch ultimately."

"Why did you take the mail?" I asked Mr. Byers. I could scarcely believe that it was I, Phillis Randolph, sitting here with these men and bravely asking questions—which they answered!

"I happened along just after John left," Mr. Byers replied. "I knew that a disorderly pile of mail would look odd to anyone who saw it, including Darien Richards if he returned just then, and at that time we were all bent on having everything appear as normal as possible, so as not to alert him. Not knowing how to put the letters away properly, I took all of them into Mr. Browning's office."

"I had been on my way there when I saw that the letters had disappeared, so I hurried off to find you, Phillis," Uncle Simon explained. "After you left me I went into the office and found him."

"Found me standing behind the door with my arms full of purloined letters, looking and feeling like a naughty schoolboy!" Mr. Byers said gleefully.

Careful, I warned myself, if you're not careful, Phillis Randolph, you'll find yourself liking this man!

"We put the letters in the boxes haphazardly," Uncle Simon said, "knowing you'd straighten everything out in short order."

I frowned. "Someone mixed the letters up once before. John, I suppose? And I remember something else that was there one day. It was a round thing made out of copper, I think."

"John left that for us too," Uncle Simon told me. "It was part of a—a sizable theft. Some Indian graves—not a mound, this time—had been looted." He glanced at Mr. Byers, who continued. "John knew I was working for the Government and that part of my work consisted of trying to stop this robbing of mounds and graves, which had suddenly become the fashion in certain areas and was beginning to get out of hand. John came to me with the information he had on some of them, and said he could identify many of the objects, if we turned them up. Then he apparently did a little sleuthing on his own, because that copper plate or gorget appeared in the post office. We didn't know until later that he had found it among Mr. Richards' effects, along with many other things taken, some of them, from private collections, which gave us more power." He glanced at Uncle Simon, and from the thin-lipped smile I observed on my uncle's face, I knew that one of the "private collections" had been his.

"What happened to it? That copper thing?" I asked. I well knew one thing that had happened to it, but I wondered how it got into the tree.

"We tried a little experiment," Mr. Byers said, looking pleased with himself. "We put it near the stall of Mr. Richards' horse. We knew he'd see it there, since he visited the horse frequently, and we chanced his not recognizing it as a piece he had already handled. We polished it, for one thing, added a dent or two. He saw it, and as we had known he would, he took it for himself. Old Jed gave me a signal, and I walked across to the stable, hoping to meet Mr. Richards, happen to notice it in his hand, and casually discuss it with him. As we drew close he stopped walking, looked up into a tree, and seemed to be most interested in its bark, or perhaps the way its branches grew. And when he turned around again, he was empty-handed."

"That's where I came into it," Gerald said with a smile. "I had taken a very real chance in visiting October House that day. I knew Darien was here, and I didn't want to be seen by him just yet, so your uncle and I hatched up a little scheme. He guaranteed to get Darien out of the place for a few hours, on the pretext of taking him to a friend's for supper, a friend who presumably could give him a great deal of information about Indian relics and all that. Then Amos and I were to search through his belongings. That was all very well, except that I made a bad mistake in the time. I thought they were to leave at five o'clock. I had an appointment at that hour myself, so I went to the stable to get my old friend Bolivar, who could take me where I wanted to go as fast as any horse could. Amos asked me to return the copper piece to John, since I was to meet with him anyway, and told me where it was. But just as I left the stable I caught a glimpse of my uncle, and it was just luck that he didn't see me at the same time. After all those months of being so careful—"

I was beginning to understand why Gerald always appeared as soon as Darien left, why Mr. Byers was usually on hand when Darien was, and perhaps other things as well.

"That was the second time I took a chance and stole my own horse," Gerald said grimly. "Earlier Darien was to have been cornered by your uncle and Amos and kept from the stable for an hour or more. But he eluded them somehow, and found Bolivar gone."

"With a poor old gray horse in his place!" I exclaimed. Everything, it appeared, had an explanation. But I had yet another surprise coming, a most unexpected bit of information that left me gasping.

"And my sister," Gerald said, "had a similar experience. We had sent her word that Darien would not visit October House for at least a fortnight, but suddenly he changed his direction and started riding straight for the place. We got word to her, with John's help, and she was able to leave in time."

"Your sister?"

"Why of course. Millicent is my sister. You didn't suspect? She said she thought you did, but of course she never mentioned it to you. She's been helping us too, has been very helpful a time or two, by the way."

I shook my head in bewilderment. All of this going on around me all this time, and me, innocent, unsuspecting, bemoaning my dull and uneventful life.

"We are getting away from the point," Uncle Simon said, cutting through my thoughts sharply. "This must all be explained to Phillis sooner or later, I know. But right now, Mr. Byers must have a few facts. Proceed, Amos."

"We have you two standing before the Indian rocks with the piece of paper in Mr. Richards' hand. Nothing else, Miss Phillis? This is most important."

I frowned. "Nothing, I'm sure of it," I told him. I could recall Darien standing there, frowning down at the paper, staring up at the rocks, talking eagerly about the arrow and its trajectory, and then his stepping so close to me that I felt frightened of him. I remembered looking down at the crumpled and soiled bit of paper he held. There was nothing else, just that.

Amos Byers sighed.

"Then, gentlemen," he said, turning to Uncle Simon and Gerald, "our work is not finished."

There was silence. Finally Uncle Simon noted my puzzled expression and spoke wearily.

"We have gone forward under the assumption that all of what we are looking for has been kept together, in a flat leather pouch which each of us has seen at one time or another. We tricked him, you might call it, into leaving it in his saddlebag while he looked at the rocks with you. Gerald watched you, as did Amos and Joseph Rock, while Carroll here searched the saddlebag for the pouch. Which he found. He removed the papers put it back where it belonged, and we assume that Mr. Richards rode away on the horse thinking his secret hoard intact."

"But then what's the matter?" I asked.

"The matter is that all of the—the papers were not there," Mr. Byers answered. "We had been so sure that they would be, that this one maneuver would net us what we wanted. But he got away, and with him some of the most important documents and pieces of evidence."

"Including the deeds to my father's land," said Gerald grimly.

"Perhaps it was divided into two parts, two pouches," I suggested, and then felt silly for having said anything so obvious.

"That it was," agreed Mr. Byers. "But Carroll is well trained, very skillful. I would stake my life that there was no other scrap of anything of interest to us on that horse."

"The most apparent place would be on his person," Uncle Simon observed. "Since he separated his infamous papers into at least two lots, that would be my guess."

Gerald nodded, scowling. "It sounds reasonable, and yet for some reason I can't explain exactly, I find it improbable. Papers in a saddlebag can be disposed of in flight, to be retrieved later. Papers on one's person are incriminating. I'm afraid my uncle is something of a coward, meaning that like most braggarts he is not terribly brave."

I thought of his mad plunges to safety. At the time I had believed them acts of courage. Now I saw I might have been wrong.

Gerald sighed. I wanted desperately to say something helpful, comforting at least. "Bolivar!" I exclaimed. "He might have left them with Bolivar."

"That possiblity has just now been explored. He used his own saddle on the horse he rode. Bolivar's stall has been searched. Nothing."

"He'll come back for Bolivar, won't he?" I asked anxiously, and when Gerald murmured, "We count on his trying," I said, "But won't he see Paladin? And know you're here?"

"He knows anyway," Gerald reminded me. "Yet I still think he's going to risk a try for Bolivar, and that makes me believe that the papers must be close to him, somewhere."

A thought struck me and, as is so often the case with me, I opened my mouth and let the words emerge on their own.

"The cut on his shoulder," I cried. "Loose wood, he said, and—well, Gerald, you said yourself ours is a well-kept stable, that it was unlikely. So maybe he—"

"Phillis, you are as bright as you are beautiful. She

could be on the right road, Byers. Bolivar's stall—that is it, of course. It must be."

"All the same," Mr. Byers said, throwing me a pleased and, I thought, congratulatory look, "we'll let Mr. Richards point the way. For more than one reason."

"And you might as well be warned, Phillis," added Uncle Simon, leaning forward across the desk, "we intend to get Darien Richards. I fancy you are fond of him, I hear most women are. But he is a scoundrel and a blackguard and—well, Mr. Byers has his reasons for wanting the man, and they are not only valid but quite legal."

My mind went to Carolina. True enough I had been smitten by Darien from the first moment, but I had lost a little of my attachment for him when he dove through the mouth of the cave, and what hero worship had remained in my mind had oozed away on the rocky slope in front of the marked rocks. He had frightened me badly and I had, in that moment, seen in him a glimmering of the evil that these men had been discussing. But Carolina—she would have nothing but pleasant memories of him, and those at long distance too, since she had scarcely more than talked to him, except for dressing that ugly wound in his shoulder.

Remembering Carolina reminded me of my duties. "If you are through with me, Uncle Simon," I suggested, standing up, "I know I'm needed."

"Run along, child," he said quickly, "but if you find yourself overtired, give it up. Carolina can manage."

Poor Carolina, always "managing." I gave Gerald a brief smile and hurried away. Someone closed the door behind me, and I heard a deep voice that made me stop in my tracks. When I first met Gerald his voice had troubled me, and now I understood. The day before his arrival I had heard just such a voice in Uncle Simon's office. So Gerald had been at October House before his official arrival, and the plot had been simmering even then. Carolina had thought Gerald reminded her of someone—that had been Darien, I realized now. The resemblance was there if you looked for it. And Millicent—why of course, she was in a way a small feminine edition of Gerald.

My mind was in a whirl, and the kitchen seemed comfortable and comforting, when I reached it. No intrigue here, no knaves to steal things, just Cottie grumbling over her stew, Carolina fussing with the trays being carried up by Ellie, Serena, and Sukey, their bare feet twinkling under their long full skirts as they ran up the stairs to the dining hall and down again. I pushed Carolina aside as she prepared to fill the heavy tureen with the fragrant stew simmering in its kettle on the crane, ladled it myself, and carried it, with some difficulty, up the stairs. Most of the guests were seated and ready, although the four I had just seen in Uncle Simon's office had not yet appeared. With Uncle Simon absent I followed a rule of the house, and served the stew myself. As I finished, Uncle Simon arrived and sat down quietly. Amos Byers and Gerald did not appear, nor did Rock and Carroll.

I was glad when the evening meal was finished. Carolina and I cleaned up in silence, and then went wearily to the weaving shed. After we had climbed into our beds, Carolina spoke.

"All right, Phillis, now tell me everything," she said sharply, and I began. It was a long story, too long, I thought, to tell when one was as tired as I was, but I felt I owed it to her. Still, I did considerable editing, not sure what it was my place to tell. She listened without comment until the very end. Then she sighed.

"It's just possible that some of these dreadful things Darien is supposed to have done exist in someone's imagination," she observed.

"But Gerald—and Uncle Simon—"

"Just the same," she said firmly, "they could be wrong. I'm sure they would not judge him without a hearing. They are fair men. They will listen to his side of it." I heard the rustle of sheets as she tucked herself in. "Good night," she said, and it was like a voice from the past. I don't know why, but I thought then that Carolina and I would never be ourselves again. I was sure I would not, not after that day. Then I shivered. Somewhere out there in the cold autumn night there was a man being hunted, hunted by other men. How would it all end?

I knew I must put it out of my head. Darien Richards was no longer my affair, surely. Gerald Richards —was. And with that more cheerful thought I turned over and went to sleep.

10

The Lifeline

There was something going on all around me, and I didn't care. Oh, of course I don't mean that, I cared deeply. But I didn't want to know about it. Whatever it was that was brewing I wished to have happen and be over and done with. I pretended to see nothing, to hear nothing, to go about my business without a thought given to the world around me.

But it was impossible not to catch a look that passed between Rock and a new guest, a man I had never seen before. Not to notice that each time Amos Byers entered the room Rock or Carroll left it. Not to reason that whatever it was that surged and ebbed and flowed around us was more or less centered in the stable. I sensed this, I tried to forget it, I made every effort to ignore it. But it was there, palpable, quivering, alive.

Above everything else I wanted it to be over. I was disenchanted with Darien, yes, but I wished him no harm. He had used me, frightened me, abandoned me —but he was still Darien Richards and I would never forget how he had looked the day he appeared at October House for the first time, nor the way he had smiled at me, nor his calling me "pretty Phillis."

So we went about our chores. Carolina was even more tight-lipped and remote than usual. I didn't know how much she knew, and I didn't dare ask. I simply did my work as efficiently and quietly as possible. October House was full, a blessing, I thought, since there wasn't much time at hand for thinking or brooding.

I don't know when I noticed it first, that faint acrid odor which crept insidiously into the air, nor have I an idea when I became conscious of it to the point where I stood still and sniffed. We were trained from birth to be fearful of fire, to be aware of smoke at all times, so that inevitably something in the very depths of our brains reached out and nudged us at the first hint.

"Smoke!" I whispered. "Smoke?" Less than an hour before, Carolina and I had finished our noontime chores, tidying up, making ready for supper later. Carolina, who said she had a headache, had left me, going down to the weaving shed to lie down for a while. I had followed her slowly, not wanting to disturb her, but at loose ends. Gerald was still about, but he was distant and withdrawn. Perhaps that was due to the unhappy circumstances of the moment, but I found myself remembering the times when I had been short with him, had even laughed at him when he paid me a compliment or said something intended to please me. I had compared him with Darien then, and could not take him seriously.

There would be no use in searching him out, but I felt I could not be alone, so at last I decided to head for the weaving shed and my own bed. It was then that the inner warning stopped me. "Smoke!" I cried it out loud this time. "Carolina, come!"

I didn't wait to find out whether or not she had heard me, I simply ran to the kitchen as fast as I could go. In the afternoon, when lamps and candles are not lighted, the kitchen is the first place one would expect to find a fire. And when I got there I discovered that I was not the only one who had sniffed the air. John, oddly enough, was there before me, and what was even stranger, Cress. A faint suspicion crossed my mind at the sight of John, but it was instantly thrust aside. John would have nothing to do with fire, he just happened to be there. Cress, who was so out of breath she must have run all the way from the slave quarters, pointed silently, and I saw the smoke circle and wreathe from the window Carolina and I had left open in the kitchen.

"Bell," said John, pointing, and I ran to the bell that stood beside the building on its iron brace, the bell that would summon everyone within earshot. I tugged at the rope with all my strength. The bell, which had never been rung in my time, had been made heavy and difficult to manage, Uncle Simon once told me, so that the children around the place would be unable to move it in play. Cress came quickly to help me, and between us we made it speak, sounding the alarm with its heavy metal tongue, and at once saw figures running to us across the field, from the stable, from every direction.

Cress let go of the rope and shouted, "Ollie, you here," and Ollie grasped the rope. Because it had been started he was able to keep the heavy tongue clanging against the bell for a time. Cress darted away, and I ran after her to the kitchen door. The place was filled with smoke. There were flames too, but not in or even near the hearth, which puzzled me even though I was not able to think very clearly. They were licking away at the pile of wood always kept by the door so that we would have an ample supply of dry wood at all times. Carolina had stormed and raged against this pile, claiming it should be outside the wall rather than in, where it interfered with our work and dirtied the kitchen, but Uncle Simon had held fast.

"If it is rained upon, it will be useless," he reminded

her. "October House must be assured of dry wood at all times." So the woodpile had remained. And now it was burning, and bits from the topmost layers of kindling were spitting and sparking, threatening to shower the kitchen with their tiny hot coals.

John went by me and into the smoke, emerging in a moment with a bucket in each hand.

"More," he said tersely, holding them out. "River."

I understood at once, and ran next door to the room where we kept large platters and bowls, tubs in all sizes, and, I remembered, a supply of buckets and pails. Cress followed me, and we took out all that were there, seven or eight in all, I suppose. The tongues of flame were licking around the doorframe of the kitchen now. We were doomed, I knew it. In a few minutes the timbers of our frame building, which at this end had been drying for more than forty years, would catch fire and then no one could stop it. October House would be no more. Tears stung my eyes, but I ran on, to have the buckets seized roughly by John.

"Go," he said, pointing. As I rounded the corner of the kitchen I blinked in amazement. There was a long line of people stretching from the corner of the house, past the weaving shed and to the river. And already buckets filled with water were being passed from hand to hand. No one spoke, no one needed to. The line worked in silence, except for slight grunts as heavy pails were given and received.

I thrust myself into a gap and had a pail given to me almost at once. Things were eerie and strange, but my panic at what was happening, what would happen, kept my mind from trying to assess the moment. I was so numb that it took me minutes to discover that the person to whom I passed each pail or bucket was Gerald. Everything was a dream or a nightmare, so why should Gerald not be in it? He wasn't real either.

Ollie left the alarm bell and, with Sugar and Spice and two or three other children, ran back and forth, carrying empty buckets to the river tirelessly. I looked ahead at the toiling line. All the slaves were there, surely. The guests too. Probably not Amos Byers, I thought, or his newfound friends. There were others though whom I didn't recognize, and I soon realized that they were Indians. Perhaps I had seen one or two of them before, here and there, I couldn't be sure. And if I had, I had no doubt been uneasy and turned away. Yet here they were, smoothly, rhythmically, helping us try to save October House.

Someone spoke to Gerald and took his place as he left the line and hurried away. My shoulders ached and the palms of my hands felt raw. I wished that I too could step out of place and rest, if even for a moment. But the buckets came on, becoming heavier and harder to grasp as the minutes went by.

Finally a voice shouted something unintelligible, and we all stopped moving. We were statues. My hands reached out for a bucket, and the man ahead—it was old Mr. Nettleton, I saw now, and how on earth had he come here?—paused as he turned with his burden. Then the voice cried out again.

"Thank you, my good friends!" it called. It was Uncle Simon, I saw, smudged and blackened and looking unlike his usual fastidious, well-brushed self. "Thank you all. The fire is out, by your good efforts. If you had not come here and worked so hard, October House would be nothing but a smoldering ruin by tomorrow. Thank you all—" His voice broke and he turned away.

The line parted. The servants walked in silence down to their quarters. The Indians melted into the forest. I felt a hand on my arm. It was Carolina.

"What happened?" she asked hoarsely. She looked as I felt, exhausted, filthy.

I shook my head and we walked toward the kitchen. John was there, and Gerald, and Uncle Simon, who was mopping his face with a dirty handkerchief and, I suspected, wiping his eyes at the same time.

"You see," Gerald was saying, "he used this." He held out a smoke-blackened firkin that I recognized as being one Cottie poured grease and drippings into. She had a tendency to use it over and over, so Carolina and I changed it now and then, using the discarded lot for making soap, and keeping the new one in the cold cellar back of the kitchen so that the grease would stay as fresh as possible.

Carolina turned to me suspiciously. "Did you leave that out?" she demanded. "It should be back in the cold room."

"I put it there, I know I did," I said quickly. I picked my way across the blackened cobblestones of the floor, strewn with ashes and partly burned pieces of wood, stippled with puddles of water, and opened the door to the cold cellar. "You see!" I cried triumphantly. "There it is!"

"Oh," said Carolina. "I'm sorry, Phillis. I wasn't thinking straight. This is the old one. I left it outside the door myself, intending to put it away later, but it slipped my mind."

"It's not your fault, Carolina," Gerald said gently. "But it was a lucky thing for our arsonist. He poured the grease on the woodpile there, and it produced the desired effect."

Just then we heard footsteps and turned. It was

Amos Byers, who was not smoke-blackened and exhausted like the rest of us. He looked clean and extremely pleased with himself.

"We have him," he reported. "My boys are with him now. If you will, Mr. Browning, we'll take the key to that cell."

Uncle Simon nodded, and they left together. Carolina, after a moment of indecision, ran out of the door and vanished in the other direction. She knew, I thought, who "him" was, just as I did. I looked up at Gerald, expecting to see some sign of victory. Instead he looked weary to the bone, and miserable. He had not, I thought shrewdly, really wanted his uncle caught. Was that possible?

I tried adding things up and said impulsively, "Gerald, it wasn't Darien who—who"—I gestured around the ruined kitchen—"who did—this?"

He nodded. "I'm afraid so," he said.

"But why?"

"To create a distraction, I suppose. We felt that Darien would never leave without Bolivar. And also that probably the rest of the papers we were looking for would have been hidden near Bolivar, in a hiding place you yourself guessed at. So we have had two men in the stable at all times, with strict instructions that they were not to leave under any conditions. He would have spotted them, and—and—well."

"But to burn down October House! Oh, Gerald!"

"I know. I suppose he didn't expect the fire to work so well. That grease being there, he might have snatched it up without thinking," Gerald said, with a tired smile. "Just a diversion, a little smoke, that was all he needed. If the men down at the stable had lost their heads and run up here to help, he would now be on his way."

"Instead," I said, not realizing I was thinking out loud, "he will be put in that dreadful cell down there." I remembered watching Sugar and Spice that day in the stable, and recalled how very real had been Spice's panic, locked into the hideous place with its stout wooden bars and no window at all. Darien, with his free spirit, his dashing past, his love of riding hard and far—how could he endure such imprisonment? No matter what he had done, the punishment was too great. Then I remembered that he had all but burned down October House, and hardened my heart.

We were very quiet at suppertime. Even the guests, who had so gallantly joined our bucket brigade and had helped to save October House, ate in silence. I myself don't remember what was served at that meal. Cottie made something, and Carolina and I saw that it reached the table above, but that's all I know. Carolina's usually immobile face was marked with pain and worry tonight, and as soon as things were cleared away I sent her to bed. I myself was too nervy to go to sleep. I felt I must find out what had happened, so I went to Uncle Simon's office, expecting to be dismissed as a naughty child. Instead he looked at me with a smile and said, "Come in, Phillis. Come in."

Again Amos Byers was there, and Gerald, and one of the new men.

"Phillis should hear," Uncle Simon said to the stranger. "She has been concerned with this almost from the beginning."

The man, another nondescript—where did Mr. Byers find these people who looked like—well, like everybody else? I wondered—gave me a slight nod and said, "We anticipated he would return for his horse." Gerald made a slight exclamation, and the man smiled thinly. "The horse he liked to think of as his," he amended. "And the papers and other things that have eluded us to date. There has been a man in the hayloft overhead every minute, and another hidden in the stable, either one of them in a position to signal to us at any time. As soon as the alarm was sounded he ran to the stall, removed a board at the front of it, and was in the process of pushing in his hand when we took him. Mr. Browning has what we wanted now."

"I searched hard for that board," Amos Byers said ruefully, "after your timely mention of the wound Richards received in the stable. Before that, I rapped and tapped all over the house and on every piece of furniture. Your uncle thought to throw me out, many's the time, I imagine."

I had seen him do that myself, and had bridled at the man's taking such liberties with our House. "But why?" I asked.

"When it became apparent that Richards planned to use this as his headquarters, it seemed logical to me that he could possibly leave papers behind for safe-keeping. Until he noted any suspicion aimed in his direction, at least. The contents of his secret hoard changed from time to time, and when he had stolen objects to sell or trade not only was it probably too great a load but he ran the risk of getting caught. At such a time he would not want all of his papers on him, we assumed."

"Mr. Byers uncovered a furniture maker on an early visit to October House," Gerald added, "who revealed that an apprentice had run away after coming into a sum of money that was sizable in the boy's mind. And the old man swore it had to do with October House, since the two had recently completed new pieces at Mr. Browning's order."

"We must not forget that it was Miss Phillis herself

who pointed a finger in the right direction," Mr. Byers said. "Well, it is over now. The man is in the cell, and he is safe enough there. We have examined it most carefully."

Uncle Simon put out a long, slim finger and touched the heavy key on his desk.

"It will be good to have this over and done with," he said. "I for one am weary of the whole thing."

"Amen," Gerald breathed fervently, and I remembered that he had told me he had been after Darien for nearly two years. What must it be like, I wondered, to pursue a man for so long? And Millicent, how had she helped? And the woman, Mrs. Mayhew, did she know all about it too?

Gerald turned to me then and said, "Phillis, you must go to bed. You look like a ghost. Come, I'll walk you down, it's late and growing dark."

I murmured something polite to the others, and Gerald and I left together. His arm was around me, and it gave me the strength I needed to put one foot before the other.

"Did Darien charm you too?" he asked me quietly. "No blame attached to you, Phillis. He had that way with him, you know."

"He—well, yes, I suppose so," I surprised myself by saying. "But, Gerald, he was so—so colorful. He had been everywhere, done everything. What woman could resist such a man?"

Gerald chuckled. "Sailed through hurricanes?" he teased me. "Fought with Jackson?"

"And spent so much time on the islands, and in Nova Scotia," I agreed.

"Do you mean," he asked, "that he didn't tell you he was in Algiers, with Decatur?"

I peered at him suspiciously in the faint light. "You

mean he didn't do all those things?"

"Oh, that Decatur story was one of his finest adventures. I hear he told it well."

"But he didn't—?" I felt foolish. I had believed every word. Every word!

"No, he didn't, my young friend. But you are not the only girl to have believed everything he told her. It is a shame, and my father said this before me, that Darien could not have employed his many talents in honest ways. Such a storyteller could be a writer. Such a swashbuckler could have carried on a vigorous and hazardous but legitimate trade. A man possessed of such tremendous energy could accomplish anything he set out to do. But he preferred to follow a crooked road, and now he has come to the end of it, in a cell in the Georgia mountains."

He sighed, and I knew that he too had some affection for his wayward young uncle. Well, he would have his beloved Bolivar back, I thought. That reminded me of something.

"Gerald, why did you ride Bolivar right at me that day?" I asked. "I thought you—or he, rather—meant to kill me."

"I was so intent on getting away, because I had to meet John and get back within the hour, that I rode as fast as I could. I've told you about my stupid error in time, and the need for my haste after I caught a glimpse of Darien. I knew if I rode in a straight line for the tree I'd keep him from seeing me. I had no idea that anyone would be out there in the field, so I was careless about looking around. When I saw you, at the last moment, my heart stopped. Literally!" He smiled at me, taking my hand. "In that crazy infinitesimal instant, I knew you were what I had been looking for. I *knew*."

My heart sang, and we walked for a bit in silence.

"But the hat!" I said suddenly, remembering. "I have never seen you with a hat on, except for that time. Did you take his, as well as his horse?"

"I occasionally wear a hat like his," he said loftily. "Thinking to confuse people, as I apparently did that day!"

That satisfied me, and we parted just outside the weaving shed. There was more to be said, but not at this moment, under the scudding clouds and with the smell of wet burned wood in the air.

I was surprised, when I climbed the steps to our room, to find that Carolina was not there. I had expected her to be sound asleep by this time. I undressed and fell wearily into bed, but sleep would not come. At last I heard stealthy steps on the stairs, and for some reason pretended sleep. Where had she been? I wondered.

When the answer to my question reached out of the black night and made itself known, I all but cried out. But no, it couldn't be. Carolina wouldn't do such a thing. Not even she would take the key from Uncle Simon's office, or find the one in the stable, and unlock the cell. Not even Carolina.

11

To Look Ahead

The air was filled with the fury of thunder and the flash of blue lightning, although it was really a calm star-spread night with no hint of either. But we were tense and tight, all of us.

Uncle Simon, whom I would have expected to pace like a restrained panther, sat at his desk and turned a pen over and over in his thin fingers. The quill hypnotized me until I felt I must look away or go mad.

Carolina, whom I would have expected to sit straight and taut, paced. Back and forth across the office, wheeling, marching, wheeling again.

As for me—well, I sat limp and suffering, not knowing where to look or what to do. Darien had been free a whole day, but the men were convinced that he was still hard by, would leave his hiding place in the dark. So they were out there now, searching, waiting, and the stars looked down on what they did. Would one kill another? Could one run away? They were like beasts, with guns instead of fangs, knives instead of claws. I thought of Darien as he had been in the beginning, so dashing, so bold. And of Amos Byers, who had bored us with his incessant questioning, but who was only doing what he had been sent to do. Of John, who was, I thought sadly, our true friend although I had misjudged him for so long. Surely he had saved my life once, and probably he more than anyone else had saved October House too. But we had—or others like us had—infringed on John's rights, disturbed his ancient gods, and who could blame him for seeking his revenge?

And Gerald. For too long I had been blind to Gerald. I had even laughed at him, and now I could see his eyes that day on the trail, turning away, angry and hurt. Perhaps it was too late for me to have discovered how I really felt about him, although with a flash of hope I remembered him saying, *In that crazy infinitesimal instant I* knew. In spite of the cold misery of the moment, the memory warmed me. Gerald had not his uncle's dash and drama, but there was much of Darien in him—his looks, the quick laughter, the blue eyes that in Gerald were clear and honest, while Darien's were bold and challenging.

How long, my restless mind went on, could we wait? How long before our nerves snapped? Carolina must have been thinking in the same way, for suddenly she stopped her restless pacing and said sadly, "This would not be happening, except for me."

"Carolina." Uncle Simon's voice was low and quiet. "You did what you did. I am not sure I would not have done the same thing, in your place."

"You, Uncle Simon?" I was fully as surprised as Carolina, who was looking at him in disbelief.

"The man did us no harm."

"He did his best to burn down—to burn down—" I gestured around me. For the rest of my life, I imagined, I would suffer a recurring nightmare of the burning of October House, although it had not happened.

"The man was desperate. He was fighting for his life, and a man in that position uses any weapon he can put his hand on. I prefer to agree with Gerald, that the fire was intended merely as a diversion. No doubt it went farther than he expected, he was in haste, but—

Well, that's not here nor there." He sighed and looked at Carolina with such compassion that I wanted to put my arms around him. Around them both. "Carolina, we are not judge and jury, but in locking him up we set ourselves up as such."

"It was that dreadful little Byers man who did it," she cried vehemently.

"As he had a right to do." Uncle Simon nodded. "An obligation, really. For my part I will be most happy to have Darien Richards apprehended elsewhere than at October House. Still, I must own I would like him apprehended. I want no further trouble here."

Carolina looked at him steadily. "Yes, of course, we must hope that—that—"

"It's the waiting!" I burst out. "It's—it's—"

"Phillis," said Uncle Simon reprovingly, but his voice was gentle and not stern.

I nodded meekly. I knew. I must be quiet. So we waited. Carolina went back to her pacing, but Uncle Simon put down his quill and linked his thin fingers together silently.

Hours or maybe only minutes later there was a sound outside. Uncle Simon jumped up and ran to the window.

"What is it?" he barked. "Who—oh, come in, come in."

Gerald? I was sure it was he, and I wanted to run to the window too, to see him, to make sure he was safe. But I couldn't move. I was tied to my chair with ropes of dread. Carolina turned toward Uncle Simon and then, with a strangely prim gesture, smoothed her hair and thrust up her chin. And walked out of the room.

In a moment Gerald was there, and with him Amos

Byers. Gerald walked directly to me.

"He is dead," he said. "He almost got away, but he was shot. Not by me, nor by Amos, but by one of Amos' men. He had a fighting chance and he almost made it." He took my hands in his and said gently, "Shall I tell Carolina, Phillis? Or will you?"

I stared at him. He knew? Knew how Carolina felt about Darien, knew that she had freed him? Which? Or both?

"I'll tell her," I said as steadily as I could. "Although," remembering her manner as she left the office just now, "although I think she already knows."

It was quite a while before I found her, huddled by the fireplace in the dining hall. The big room was full of shadows and ghosts and memories, and it made me shiver.

"Carolina," I began, not having yet made up my mind how to break it to her.

"He's dead, isn't he? I knew it. I expected it. But there have been no more—no more—"

"Everyone else is back," I said carefully. "Including the indestructible Mr. Byers."

That coaxed a wan smile from her.

"Go back to Gerald," she said. "I'll be all right. I expected nothing, you see, and that's what I got. Nothing. It was, as you said, the waiting."

"And the—hoping."

"There is always that. Or there was. Phillis, I am not at all sorry I let him out of the cell. That way he had a fighting chance, and I'm sure that's all he really wanted. I'm glad I gave him a few hours of freedom, and that the last minutes of his life were lived in hope, not in a cage like an animal. Go on, Phillis, leave me."

I didn't want to go, but I knew she wished me to. So, with a last awkward hug I went back to Gerald.

Uncle Simon had shut himself up in the office with Amos Byers and probably another man or two, and Gerald was waiting in the passageway.

"Official reports," he said, gesturing toward the closed office. "They will do nothing to Carolina, by the way. That has been settled. How is she taking it?"

"She'll be all right." That was true, I knew, but it was also true that she would have many sorrowful hours before it was over in her heart.

"We'll take care of her," Gerald promised me. "You have depended on her long enough."

I stared at him. I had never thought of it that way, but he was right.

Gerald took my arm and propelled me outside and to the kitchen.

"This may not be the time, nor is it exactly the ideal place," he said, looking around him wryly, "but we must talk about the future."

I gazed at him blankly.

"As you know, I've been looking for land," he said, pretending not to notice my expression. "And after searching all over the state I have found just what I want. It is here, adjacent to October House."

I smiled happily. He would be close, and I would have a chance to start over, to make no mistakes that would affect our relationship.

"And at the same time I have been looking for something to do," he went on. "I have, since my father's death, managed our place on the islands, but my sister, Millicent, is marrying our next-door neighbor, Robert Graves, and he will take over our holdings and add them to his own, with my blessing, of course. That, in a sense, pushes me out in the cold. So I will become a landowner in these mountains, and your uncle has agreed to let me assist him in the management of October House."

"Uncle Simon has—"

"He finds it taxing, for a man his age, and welcomes a younger back to carry part of the burden. For that matter, he admits he is not entirely suited to the role of innkeeper in some ways. He likes the figures and the keeping of books, and has a knack for the planning and requisitioning of foods and such, but unfortunately he does not enjoy mingling with the guests."

I ducked my head at that. It was most apparent, but I had never thought of it as a defect in Uncle Simon's character.

"Most of all, he needs a strong hand in the management of the slaves," Gerald went on. "He confesses that he has dropped too much of the responsibility for the overseeing of the household chores on Carolina's shoulders. And I strongly suspect that Carolina, because of her age and lack of experience, has found it easier to do much of the work herself. With your help," he added, smiling. I gaped at him. Of course it was true. Carolina's way of ordering the servants around left much to be desired. Cottie, for example, walked all over her far too often.

"My father," Gerald continued, "had a large household, larger than this although it was that of a private family. I have had the experience needed. I promise you that. If Carolina wishes to remain as housekeeper, and I hope she will, she will do none of the work, just oversee. I'll make sure of that." He smiled happily. "Phillis, I have plans for October House which will see an increase in the size of its staff, among other things. Now, I suspect you would just as soon never see the inside of October House again—"

"But it's my home! The only one I remember!"

"Well, I put that badly. Just as soon not see the daily chores that come with its maintenance, I meant. So on the land I have bought there is a house, not far from here, owned by a family named Phillips, who are moving down to the coast."

Phillips! Could he mean the house owned by Sterling Phillips, who married the Hawley girl? That had always been my notion of a perfect house, because it was trim and gracious. It seemed to me a private, personal house, and it stood on the edge of the Oktobee River where a branch joined it, giving a most delightful vista.

"So, unless you have an objection, we will live there," Gerald went on. "I plan to add a small wing, and that will be for Carolina for as long as she wants it. She might in time meet a guest of suitable age and means!" He stopped talking and grinned at me. "Am I going a little too fast for you, Phillis?"

"A little," I admitted.

"I'm sorry. Well, I think I have said enough for now. Except to add that Millicent is overjoyed at the prospect of having you for a sister-in-law. In fact, she came here not so much in the line of duty, so to speak, as to satisfy herself that you were good enough for her only brother. You passed the test with flying colors. Now she's looking forward to our visiting them on the island, and—"

"Gerald," I said faintly. *"Much* too fast!"

"And there's no hurry, is there! Well, it's an enchanting prospect, our future." Then he frowned. "There is of course one thing I don't like. If this rumor of gold persists, and it seems to crop up more and more frequently, the peace and quiet of our mountain world may be shattered. In that event we may decide to change our plans. Which we can do at any time. I really don't like to look ahead, just now. If there is gold in any quantity around here, it will bring the worst elements into the area. Greed makes fools of men. Greed—that was at the bottom of everything Darien did. And there will be others like him. In that case, we'll move along." He looked at me anxiously. "Would you be willing?"

I looked into his eyes for the first time since he started talking. I didn't have to hunt for the words.

"I'll be willing to go anywhere with you, Gerald," I told him, and knew it to be true.

And in the silent kitchen of October House, he kissed me for the first time.

Author's Note

October House is a completely fictional hostelry, based loosely on Traveler's Rest, that fascinating old place in Toccoa, Georgia. The Oktobee River and Falls are also my invention.

Other landmarks of the area have been borrowed and sometimes distorted for my purpose—Dahlonega, where just after the time of my story there was a genuine gold rush, this country's first; Track Rocks; the multitude of waterfalls and trails, vistas and mountains and valleys, everything that captured the imagination of a transplanted New Englander on a few brief visits to a beautiful part of our world.